His Thawing Heart

Zoe Lec

Obligatory Disclaimer

It must be mentioned that this is, in fact, a work of fiction. Any resemblance to people or places is purely coincidental.

All rights reserved. No part of this book may be reproduced, scanned or distributed in any printed or electronic form without permission, except for the use of brief quotations in a book review. Please purchase only authorized editions.

All songs, song titles, and lyrics mentioned in the novel are the property of the respective songwriters and copyright holders.

The views and ideas in this work do not necessarily reflect those of the photographers and models used on the cover.

His Thawing Heart and all properties within Copyright © 2020 Zoe Lee Books and Foolish Endeavors, LLC

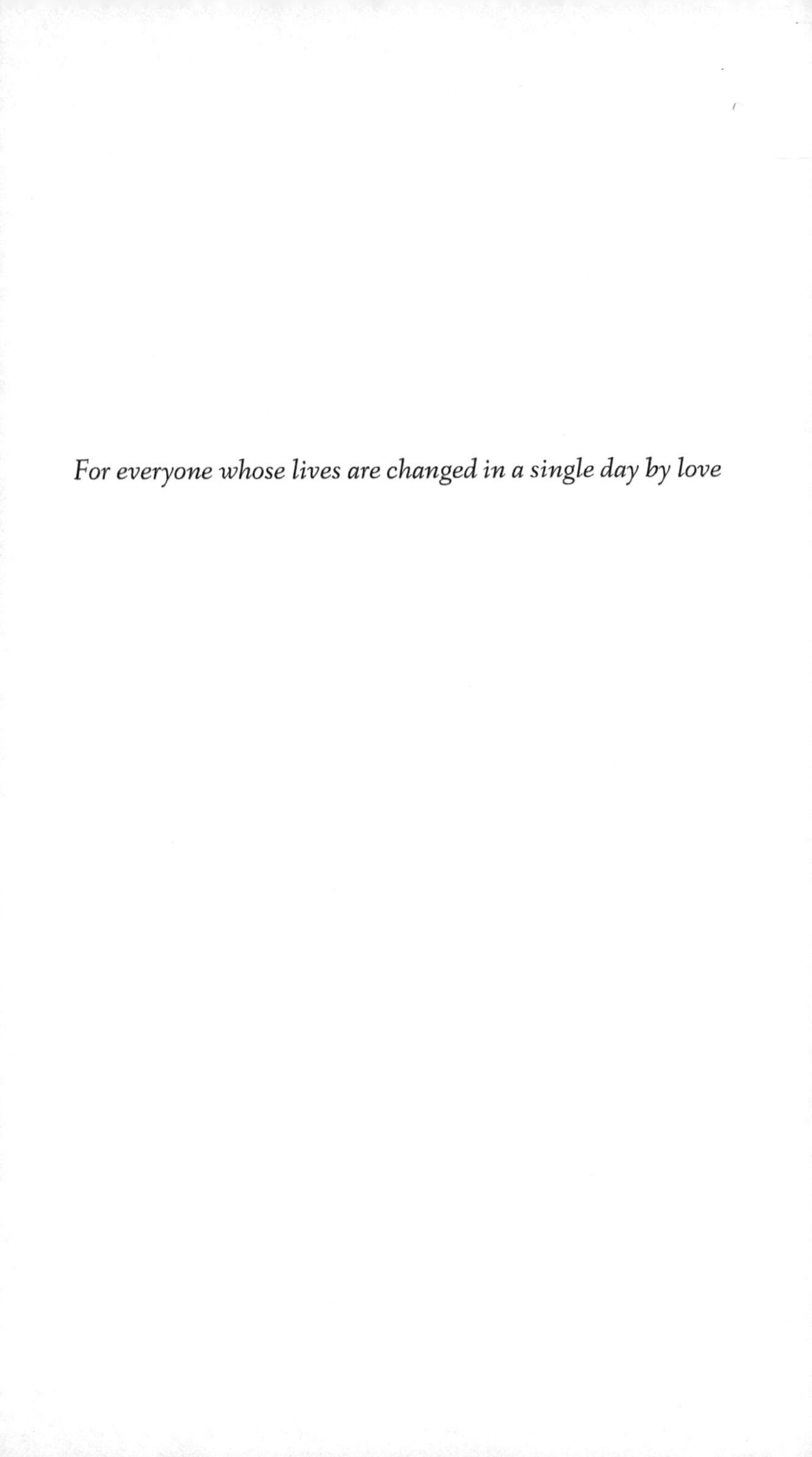

For everyone whose lives are changed in a single day by love

Chapter One

Trentham

This whole week had been a royal shit show.

I flipped up my coat collar and shivered, eyeing all of the new notifications pouring in now that I'd turned my phone on after my three-hour flight from Chicago to Aspen. They looked like harmless little white digits in blue bubbles telling me that people had contacted me in some way. But they were miniature bombs designed to mess up my life if they were set off. This was supposed to be the beginning of months of relaxation after a year of non-stop touring, but yesterday morning, I'd woken up in London to digits in the hundreds.

Dallas Birch, longtime squeeze of Downbeat rhythm guitarist Becker Trentham, marries mystery man in secret Lake Tahoe wedding! Becker Trentham disappears after boyfriend, TV actor Dallas Birch, marries some other guy!

Irritation with Dallas flared, worse than usual since his choices were causing me extra grief , so I called Xavier, one of my few best friends and the frontman of our band Downbeat.

"*Dude,*" Xavier hissed when he picked up.

"I know," I groaned. "I don't want to talk about that. I have another problem."

"I'm going to tell it like it is: your life's a soap opera."

I scrubbed one cold hand over the knit hat I wore. "Yeah. So look, I'm in Aspen for a thing tomorrow night. I booked a room at the same hotel as the thing, but I can't go there now. There's going to be paps everywhere trying to get a pic of me brokenhearted or some crap."

"Have you talked to Kayla yet?"

Kayla was Downbeat's publicist, and I loved her to death, but I hated talking to her as a musician to a publicist. Some of this was my fault for ever dating an aspiring actor. I wouldn't trade our music career or the fans for anything, but the rest of it sucked.

"Not yet. But I will, no need to gasp dramatically," I said over Xavier's noise. I screwed up my face, not wanting to ask this next question, but I didn't have any other ideas. "Listen, does your brother still live in the area? I'm not canceling my thing, but I gotta lie low for a night."

My phone chimed and I pulled it away from my ear to see that Xavier was inviting me to a video chat. Swearing under my breath, I picked up, because he'd only try again.

"What, you miss my face already?" I mocked him.

"Nope, but I have to see how constipated you look while you beg for my help."

His shit-eating grin pissed me off and I flipped him the bird. "Why are you like this?"

He snorted and reminded me, "You're the one who's allergic to happiness. How are you ever going to survive a night with my brother? You do remember Enzo is *always* happy, right?"

Xavier's brother and I had only met a few times, but that was the reason I wasn't happy about asking for this favor. I loved music and liked my life fine, but people who were always in a good mood and always looking at the bright side made me grind my teeth.

I swiped a hand over my face. "I'm in a bind here, man."

Xavier's expression sobered and he nodded, asking, "Are you sure you don't want to talk?"

"Not a chance, Xav. Can you please cut me a break, call Enzo, and get back to me? I'm freezing my nuts off standing in a shadowy corner of the airport parking lot. It's *January*."

"Okay, okay."

He rolled his eyes and hung up, and I fiddled with my phone to keep my hands busy.

Less than five minutes later, it rang.

"It's your lucky day," Xavier said cheerfully. "He's leaving on a ski vacation tomorrow, but he's around tonight. I"ll text you his address and his number. You rented a car, right?"

"I can get there," I assured him, even though there was no way in hell I'd rented a car. I hated driving on a good day, but in winter in a mountain town? No, thanks. "I owe you one."

With a laugh, Xavier told me, "I owe you fifty, so it's cool. Please don't, like, murder Enzo."

"No promises," I grunted, and hung up so I could order a ride.

The app said no one could get here for about twenty minutes, so I took a deep breath and called Kayla. Best to get it out of the way now, because I knew she was already working on how she thought I should respond. Part of me resented that I'd probably do everything she said, like I always did, because I wasn't one to take orders, but she hadn't steered me wrong yet.

"Finally," Kayla exclaimed when she answered. "You

landed an hour ago! I've got a statement all drafted and emailed to you. All you have to do is okay it and I'll post it for you."

"How? You don't even know what happened," I pointed out.

There was a pause before she said, "Please. Six months ago you went to your doctor and got tested, even though you had your annual checkup less than two months before that."

"How do you know that?" I demanded in a sharp tone. "That's a serious privacy breach."

"The results got sent to Hank by mistake, since you have to get checkups while you're on tour. He called me to keep an eye out and make sure there wasn't an issue," she summarized.

Hank was our manager and a caretaker by nature, so it didn't surprise me. "Damn it."

"I've known you a long time, so I know you weren't cheating," Kayla went on, without bothering to apologize for overstepping since Hank had asked her to. "So Dallas did. *Or* you broke up but he convinced you to play pretend since he's got a new series premiering in a week. Either way, he did something selfish and I'm going to handle it so you don't have to."

Feeling a headache start to brew, I didn't bother to confirm how accurate her estimate of what had happened was, and said instead, "Okay, I'll read the email in a bit and let you know."

"So which is it?" she demanded after a second of silence.

"Doesn't matter," I sighed. "That fire burned out a long time ago anyway. I gotta go."

I rolled my shoulders, trying to relieve some of the pressure building, and grabbed my suitcase, then went over to the taxi stand where the car was supposed to pick me up.

A group of younger women were waiting in a clump nearby, gossiping and looking like models in their rich girls' ski trip boots and shiny puffy coats, no hats to mess up their hair.

Angling away from them, I was glad winter fashion hid my more recognizable features.

Just when my nose and fingers in my pockets were starting to go numb, my ride arrived and I climbed into the back of a big SUV, slumping against the seat as the heat blasted me.

"Hey," the driver said, barely tossing me a look in his rearview, before he confirmed my destination and started driving. "First time in Aspen?" he asked a minute later.

"I think so."

He laughed. "Most people remember if they've been here before or not."

"I'm not most people," I replied, then put in my earbuds to give him a big fat hint I wanted to be left alone. I put on a meditation thing Hank had suggested. I didn't have anger issues, but my size made my gruffness intimidating and easy to read as anger. Listening to the meditation shit was good for clearing out all of the bullshit I had to deal with, so I liked it.

By the time the SUV pulled over in front of a wood complex, I felt like all of the shitty things that had happened over the last week were far away from me. Tonight all I'd have to worry about was the urge to pop the bubble of magical fairyland happiness Enzo lived in.

Chapter Two

Enzo

"Okay, babies, it's time to get serious," I said to my two dogs and one cat, perched on the coffee table while they sprawled out lazily across my couch. "We're having a guest tonight."

Slush pushed his nose into his cushion and somersaulted onto his back.

"A very famous guest," I added.

Eloise slowly, deliberately dug her back feet into Bruiser's butt, pushing him away.

"So I'm going to have to vacuum," I concluded.

All three of them jerked their animal faces over to me immediately at the word *vacuum*, and when I stood up, they all jumped off the couch and scrambled into my bedroom.

Smiling, I followed and shut the door, then put on some action movie and got to work cleaning up. The condo wasn't dirty, exactly, but I'd been preoccupied the last month or so, so there were furry dust bunnies under the furniture and the toilet was due for a scrubbing.

I wasn't really *nervous*, or I wasn't nervous about having a famous musician over, since my brother was one too. It was more that this particular famous musician was... kinda scary, if I was being honest with myself. He was hulking and always looked so edgy and fashionable. When he sat down, he made chairs groan in protest. The flat, too cool to be exasperated look he'd leveled on me (and a lot of reporters) before made me feel like prey.

But this was going to be great and I could never have said no anyway, not after Xavier had told me that the press was hounding Trentham over relationship gossip. No one deserved that treatment unless they were involved in something people had an actual *right* to know about. Unless Trentham was sleeping with a married senator or something, they didn't.

Once the condo was clean, but not spotless like I'd stressed about it, I was a sweaty mess, so I hopped in the shower. Knowing he would be here in less than twenty minutes, I scrubbed down real quick, then got dressed in black sweats and a dark green thermal shirt.

It was about six when my door shook in its frame with the force of the knocks on it.

Squaring my shoulders, I told myself, "You can do this. Be cool, Enzo."

With a tug on my thermal, I flung open the door and exclaimed, "Hey, Trentham!"

The giant looming in the hall grunted and shouldered past me, almost knocking me over.

As I shut the door, I heard Bruiser and Slush barreling across the floor, their nails clicking and scritching wildly as they came to investigate the intruder. "Oh, I hope you like..."

Trentham's blunt-boned face cracked into a smile as he dropped onto his haunches and held out his hands for my dogs to attack with licks. "Hey, cuties," he cooed to them.

"The Corgi is Bruiser and the Pointer is Slush," I said proudly, relieved he wasn't trying to edge away from my doggies. People who hated animals were the worst. "Slush is two and Bruiser is five. I have a cat too, Eloise, but she's too cool and disdainful to greet new people."

"I can't have pets with how much I travel," he said, rubbing his hands on Slush's tummy when she rolled over to present it to him, wriggling gleefully, and I felt a little hot all over.

So I'd known there was something worth considering in what Ariane had said during our breakup, but oh man, I had not expected to have a hot flash watching a man pet my dogs.

Okay, I thought, let's save the deep thoughts for any time but now.

I smiled brightly and told my brother's best friend, "I'm sorry there's paparazzi on your tail, but I'm happy to help you hide. A day later, and you would've had to get my spare key from Mrs. Manzanillo next door, and I swear, no one can talk longer about the weather."

Gently pushing the dogs away, he got to his feet and unlaced his boots, kicking them onto the rubber mat for snowy footwear. When he caught me staring at him, he narrowed his eyes at me and said like it was an accusation, "I forgot how different you are from Xavier."

A flash of insecurity lit me up even though I'd heard that a million times before. It was what happened when your older brother—half-brother if you wanted to get technical—was a charming, really handsome man with a giant, magical voice whose band got famous too.

"We have tons in common," I replied with a carefree grin. "First, we both talk a ton."

"I'm aware," Trentham said, and nope, I hadn't known a tone could shrivel balls before.

"Uh," I said eloquently, "are you hungry? I haven't eaten yet and it is dinner-time so…"

As if he were an exotic dancer in Antarctica, he undid each button on his jacket with sure flicks of his fingers, pausing to let it hang open and frame his midline like a spotlight.

I collapsed against a bookcase from the *sexiness* of him basically *stripping*. There was no way I could have ever pulled off that move, but damn could I still appreciate it.

"Yeah, what kinds of food can you order in around here?"

"A-anything you want," I stuttered as he flung his jacket back off his shoulders so that it slid off his body in one smooth move, the red silk lining like flames.

He tossed it at the coat hooks, where it landed perfectly, then pulled off his knitted beanie to uncover, not the bleached undercut I'd last seen, but light brown layers along his jawline.

"I could go for some burgers and fries," he suggested.

Nodding like an idiot, I tore my eyes off him and groped for my phone. "There's a great place, let me pull up the menu and then you, ah, just… Never mind, you know how to order."

One eyebrow lifted, judging me, but he came closer and took my phone. His hands were really big—his *everything* was really big—so he was very careful and deliberate as he used his thumb to scroll and tap out his selections. I wondered how he typed with those things.

Once he was done, he handed it back to me and I tapped something, no idea what but I wasn't too picky about food at all, and then submitted the order. "It'll be here in thirty."

"Good," he said, and started to sweep his dark blue eyes around the condo.

It wasn't much, a kitchen and living room combination with some plants hanging from the windows so my pets wouldn't eat them, then a short hall with the bathroom and bedroom. But Aspen was an expensive city and while my job was awesome, I couldn't afford much more. I kept it bright with landscape photos of the awesome mountains right outside and some pumpkin-colored throw pillows an ex-girlfriend had given me for my birthday.

"You'll have to sleep on the couch," I blurted out as his eyes fixed on the short hall.

With a shrug, he said, "I've been sleeping mostly on a tour bus, so no problem."

"Right, of course," I said. "So, uh, how was the tour? I haven't talked to Xav much lately."

His eyes came back to me as he crossed his arms. "Exhausting."

"Well, that's why you're all taking a break, huh?" I encouraged him. "Everyone needs time to recharge and feel like a normal guy for a while, Xav's always told me. He's coming for a visit in February sometime, I can't wait to see him. He always brings me really good presents."

Trentham nodded and cracked his knuckles, then went over to the couch and sat, patting his enormous thighs to encourage the dogs, who'd trotted behind him at his heels, to hop up.

Wishing I could nuzzle into those thighs exactly like my dogs were, I shook my head and took a seat on the other end of the couch. I pulled up a knee and watched some of the tension melt out of his wide shoulders as he petted the dogs some more, and I got curious again.

"So, uh, what's with the paparazzi now?"

A sour look came over his face and he said, "My boyfriend got married over the weekend."

"Man, people are such dicks about polyamory!" I said indignantly. "Anyway, how was it?"

Trentham's head lifted slowly until he could stare at me incredulously.

"What?" I asked, actually glancing down to make sure I looked normal.

"We weren't polyamorous," he bit out. "I had no idea he was seeing someone, let alone…"

My face fell and I bit my lip. "That's… Okay, yeah, that's not… the best." His mouth pinched and I bet if his hair wasn't hanging over his jaw, I would've seen it twitching. "Are you the type of guy who wants a pep talk about how you're amazing and can do so much better? Or do you want to hear all about my most recent mishap in love and dating? It's a doozy."

"I definitely don't want to talk about my shit or listen to some encouragement from someone who barely knows me," he denied.

His eyebrows scrunched together and it looked like he was going to ream me out for being insensitive or stupid or something. But after a couple quick, hard heartbeats, they relaxed and he gave what seemed like a reluctant chuckle. "Sure, why not? Tell me this *doozy*."

If I was honest, I would've rather spent the time until food got here trying to cheer him up. I'd rather say whoever had cheated on him—and then married someone else without giving him the heads up—sucks, and that there was someone way better for him out there.

But I'd offered, so I readjusted my glasses even though they were fine, and began, "Ever since my very first date, I've always had a girlfriend. I love being in a relationship, I always thought I was really good at it. Sometimes it was a few months, sometimes a few years. There are only a couple exes I didn't stay friends with, and one of those moved away so there wasn't a chance to stay connected anyhow. I love hugs and presents and planning for the future."

"I never would've guessed that," Trentham interjected in the driest tone ever.

Laughing, I held my hands up. "I know, it's cheesy and not... not the manliest."

"Manliness is fake, but go on," he ordered.

I grinned at him, jumping a little when Eloise landed on my lap without warning. I snuggled her up on my chest, her paws kneading my shoulder joint, and stroked her ears. "I was never that guy who was always after sex or always thinking about it, but I never felt anti-sex at all either, so I just figured I was, I don't know, more romantic than all that."

"Ugh," Trentham grunted, mouth twisting.

Knowing what he was going through, I let that go.

"But my last girlfriend Ariane said we weren't in sync about sex and stuff," I explained, not embarrassed at all. Even though Trentham seemed like the kind of guy who never talked about sex, but was awesome at having it. "She wanted to try to figure it out. It was super sweet, she went through this whole kind of checklist to see if I'm maybe asexual or gray ace."

"Okay," he said, and now he looked a little intrigued, maybe.

"None of the things we read and talked about felt like it fits me though."

"So maybe you two weren't sexually compatible. It happens all the time, even when two people are really into each other on all the mental-emotional levels," he pointed out.

Eloise stuck the tip of her tail up my nose and I sneezed it out violently, making the dogs leap up and bark. Trentham blinked in surprise, while I reached for a tissue to try to blow out all the cat hair in my nose, grumbling in annoyance, "Eloise, come on, we've talked about this."

The buzzer sounded and I bounced up, leaving Eloise to stalk off to my bedroom.

"I got it. You probably don't want to show your face to a stranger anyway, huh?"

I answered the door, then looked down when there weren't two dogs trying to wriggle their way out to attack the delivery kid. Confused, I twisted around and saw Trentham in the kitchen, holding both of them like footballs under one arm, casual as you please, while he opened cabinets until he found the plates. Something warm flickered in my chest, and I was grinning like a maniac as I turned back to the delivery kid and took the food finally.

"Thanks," I told her. "Have a good night."

"It's going to storm, I heard," she muttered glumly.

"Stay safe!" I called cheerfully as she headed down the hall, closing the door.

Trentham had put the dogs down and found plates, napkins, and some beer. "Bring that over here," he called in a gruff voice. "I'm starving and I want to hear the end of your story."

It wasn't every day that someone like Trentham cared what I had to say, so I hurried over and untied the plastic bag, then pulled out the wrapped burgers and cups of fries.

We put them on the plates, he picked up the beers in one of his hands, and we went back to the couch.

"Off," I commanded the dogs, and they gave us mournful looks before complying.

"Don't leave me hanging, you're trying to make me feel better here or some shit," Trentham prompted after we'd each taken our first bites.

I swirled a couple fries in ketchup and shoved them in my mouth to buy a few seconds.

"So she says it's cool if that's how I am about sex," I continued with a small sigh. "But she's got different needs. She says she hopes I meet someone great who's got the same thing going as me. And on her way out, she suggests if I don't, I should try men."

Suddenly Trentham was shaking, his face reddening, and for a split second of panic, I thought he was choking. But then, once he'd gotten down the burger in his mouth, he was roaring with laughter.

I'd never seen him do that before, so my mouth fell open in awe. It was a beautiful sound, ringing, fast bursts of *ah-ha-ha* while his whole body rocked with it.

When he'd gotten it all out, he wiped his eyes and sucked in a big breath.

"What did you do then?"

Shrugging, I answered, "I thanked her for the idea and started scoping out dudes, man."

That made him choke again, eyes going wide in surprise. "Wait, really?"

I chuckled and replied, "Yeah, really. I'd never felt like there was anything wrong in my relationships, they just weren't my soulmates, you know? And it's too bad because a lot of my exes are super amazing women. Still, if they're not a soulmate, there's no reason to drag it out."

"There's a big space between saying they weren't right, and saying the answer is men."

Now I scowled at his narrow-mindedness. "Why are you shocked? Aren't you bi?"

"Sure, but I didn't start fucking dudes because I hadn't found the perfect woman."

"I hear all that cynicism," I huffed, waving a finger at him, "but it's not going to put a dent in my optimism, Trentham. She didn't say it like some meanie implying that the only reason we weren't five-alarm hot between the sheets is because I'm actually gay."

He grunted in disbelief and retorted, "Sounds like it to me."

I rolled my eyes and ate some more, then washed it down with beer.

Since he was still looking at me like he thought I was crazy, I waved away the question of Ariane's intentions. "Either way, men are *really* doing it for me now that I'm thinking about it."

"*Thinking* about it."

After polishing off my food, I slouched back into the corner of the couch and chirped, "That didn't sound like a question, but I'll answer anyway. Yeah, thinking. I'm not some hot shit famous musician who can walk around wearing leather and get numbers thrown at him."

"Is that really how you think it works?"

I snickered and confirmed with a straight face, "Absolutely."

He tipped his beer bottle up, thick neck working as he finished it too.

My mind helpfully supplied me with similar shots from all of the gay and bisexual porn I'd treated myself to in the past month. Yeah, he was going to fit into my masturbation montage *very* well...

"Men are definitely getting me hot and bothered," I went on, still so elated by this new revelation. "And how amazing is that to find out about myself? I don't know what it means at all, but if it might expand the number of potential soulmates, wow, I want to know for sure. I want to see if I love dating men as much as I love dating women. And I want to see if I'm mostly super romantic with an occasional urge to make love with men, the way I am with women, or if it's totally different. No matter what, it's going to be so great!"

Trentham scrubbed his hands over his face, his blond stubble rasping against his rough palms audibly, and groaned, "Holy shit, you're just so... young, and... *happy* and *earnest.*"

"Being excited about finding a soulmate isn't naive," I argued hotly. "I know that's what you meant by young and earnest. I might be a decade younger than you, but I'm twenty-five."

"I'm thirty-nine, but who's counting," he muttered into his hands.

"Are you telling me that there isn't a single, eensy weensy bit of a thrill in your heart at the knowledge that you're single again? That you can go out there and find someone who's going to love you and be faithful and not run off to marry someone else behind your back?"

He glared at me and said, "Baby, I'm thrilled Dallas is out of my life for good and I'm thrilled to be single, but it's definitely not because I want to find my fuckin' *soulmate.*"

Baby?

Bruiser barked and scratched at the doormat, and Slush lifted her head out of the water bowl and yipped back, her tail wagging. "I, uh, I need to take the dogs out. You hang out here."

Without waiting for a response, I went to put on my boots, coat, and hat, clipped on the dogs' leashes, and shoved a few plastic baggies in my coat pocket. As I backed out the door, fumbling to tug my gloves on, I glanced up to find Trentham giving me some new look I'd never seen on him before. Whatever it was, I thought as I shut the door and let the dogs drag me along towards the snow-covered lawn behind my complex, it made my pulse race.

Chapter Three

Trentham

As soon as Enzo and the dogs were gone, I shot off the couch and went into the bathroom. Yeah, I had to go, so I did, but then I scowled at my reflection while washing my hands. Xavier and I had met about fifteen years ago. He'd been at Juilliard with another original bandmate, Seth, and I'd been a bouncer and a professional poker player. Since we were in New York, I hadn't met Enzo until he was a teen, and then I'd only seen him a couple times since, maybe the summer after high school and around the time he turned twenty-one.

So in my mind, he'd still been this baby-faced, scrawny weirdo.

But the Enzo out walking his dogs was a *man*. Still more cute than hot, but I had always appreciated something less flashy, so cute turned me on way more than hot could dream of.

He was a bit under six feet with dark brown hair and bronze skin pale in the winter. His body was casual, regular, healthy with gentle muscle definition like he hiked a lot, not hit the gym. The glasses gave him a sweetness that wasn't my usual thing, but the way he touched them all the time kept drawing my attention to the big, soft light brown eyes behind them.

I wasn't the man who hunted or pursued, but Enzo was just so damn... seducable.

I'd had great experiences being guys' first time with another man. It was satisfying to be up for whatever they'd been fantasizing or curious about and make it good for them. And Enzo was so painfully over the moon about that, I could blow his mind. Then tomorrow morning, I'd head out with a wave, and he'd learn this idea of *soulmates* he clung to was nonsense.

With my mind made up, I settled back onto the couch and waited.

He and the dogs came back in a little later, drifts of heavy snow on his shoulders and hat and matting down the dogs' fur. He dried them off with a towel, then stripped off his gear.

"Whew! The snow's like crystals out there, it's gorgeous," he enthused as he sat next to me. "Where were you before? Because if you're feeling the jetlag, I can hang out in my room so you can crash, it's not a big deal. I should go to bed early anyway to be rested for my trip."

I let a different, secret smile unfurl across my face, running a hand through my hair to shamelessly flex my muscles and show off my face unframed by my hair. "Nah, I'm up."

That voice, a little lower and raspier than usual, made him gulp and shift around. I stretched my arm out along the top of the couch, my arm touching his shoulder lightly.

"I don't think we'll have the same taste in movies, but you're the guest, so you could pick one out?" he offered, the words coming a little quicker than usual as he tried to act unaffected.

Something sparked in my chest and skipped down lower to between my thighs.

"Choose what you want," I told him, letting my fingertips drift over the back of his neck, so light it might have been an unconscious accident. "Might not make it through anyway."

His body twitched and he lunged forward to grab up the remotes.

This was *fun*, I realized. I hadn't had sex in a few months, and I appreciated the way he gripped the remote even though it wasn't really that phallic of an object. I kept my eyes on his profile as he searched for a movie, and I watched his throat work and felt his neck arch the tiniest fraction, seeking out my touch again. His eyes were hazy behind his glasses, his thick eyelashes fluttering as he tried to concentrate, and then he suddenly tossed the remote aside.

"Are you going to make a move or what?" he demanded, twisting to face me head on.

"I can be patient," I replied, because I loved the slow build of tension, my cock firming up in my jeans and throbbing with every heartbeat to get free.

"And you're looking for something that lasts, not screwing around with a virtual stranger," I had to add, since as seducable as he was, Enzo wasn't a virtual stranger, he was my best friend's little brother.

He huffed out a laugh and his thighs spread and closed restlessly, the heavy sweatpants fabric doing almost nothing to hide the swell of his erection. "I don't know for sure if I like men like that. I'm not going to ask a guy out before I even know I'll want to be with one."

"Looks like you already know." I ghosted my other hand over the swell in his sweats.

"Ohh, I already know that I like the idea," he agreed in a shaky voice. "But I—it's like you can get off to some weird porn, but you're not really sure you want that in reality. Right?"

I hummed in consideration. "I'm not into porn much. I have a *really* great imagination."

"Or you have like twenty years of kinky memories in your spank bank," he mumbled.

That surprised a laugh out of me, and I rewarded him by stroking up his thigh. "Can't deny there were some wild times. But you're right, you'll never know until you do it yourself."

His gaze dropped from my face down my body, and I wondered what he was thinking. It wasn't perfect anymore —it got harder to stay in shape, especially on tour, the older I got.

When he swallowed hard, I figured it might not be perfect, but it was still blatantly male.

"Seems like an opportunity I shouldn't ignore," he whispered, licking his lips.

"Was that permission?" I countered while I spread my hand over the back of his neck.

He made a little noise of shock and pleasure and then tumbled forward, hands landing on my shoulder and pec, to kiss me.

I had been expecting it to be overeager and fumbling, but he surprised me by swiping his tongue over my bottom lip before pressing it inwards and my lips yielded without thought.

My fingers curled into his neck tighter as he stroked over my chest and shoulders, then hung onto my biceps while diving deeper into my mouth. He shuffled in and swung one knee over one of my thighs so he could get closer, his body giving off so much heat and filling the air with his smell, snow and something smoky.

When he settled his weight onto my thigh, his erection angling into the crease of my hip, I eased away from his mouth. "Oh, baby, do you even know what you're asking for?"

"This is so hot," he gasped back, grinning at me and squeezing my arms, testing their strength. "Can I suck your dick? Or maybe you can top me, if you're into that?"

My eyebrows rose at his boldness, but I tipped my chin up confidently. "Have at it."

Chapter Four

Enzo

None of my fantasies compared to having Becker Trentham sprawled out on my couch like he was a king, giving me consent to use his giant, beefy body to confirm I was bi.

But that didn't mean I hesitated for a millisecond.

Taking immediate advantage of the way he'd raised his chin, I leaned in to suck and lick over his jaw and neck. I wasn't sure if he was bored or just into gay sex newbies or what, but I was sure tonight was all he was offering. So I wasn't going to waste time wondering if I was doing it right or if it was as good for him as it was for me. No, I was going to grind my dick against him and grope his chest and waist and shoulders with endless glee and leave hickies.

But I quickly missed his mouth, so I trailed back up and kissed him again.

He was so much bigger all around than any woman I'd been with, and his mouth seemed huge too, sucking in my tongue. All I could think was, *I want him to unhinge that jaw around my dick.* It was a little unnerving because I hadn't lied, I really was into lovemaking. I'd never been into blow jobs because I loved kissing, I loved that intimacy while bodies blended together.

My hands pushed under his shirt, grabbing onto his waist, and he shifted, draping one thigh over my bent knee so that I could feel his dick against my balls. I convulsed with the strength of his dick and the rest of his body, slabs of muscle under a delicious little layer of stockiness. When I raked my hands in and up, I found out he had body hair, crinkly and rough, and I moaned into his mouth, grinding more frantically against him, aching to go further.

He swiveled his hips and wrapped his arms around me, taking over the kiss to plunge his tongue into my mouth, every now and then dragging it over my teeth and palate.

"*Becker*," I whined. "I can't think. I—I'm *so close*, help me, oh my God—"

I clamped my mouth shut and squeezed my eyes tight, too overwhelmed to go on.

Then I was being carried, feeling like I was floating while still anchored by his hands, and distantly I heard him ordering the pets out of my bedroom, then the door shutting.

"Where are your condoms and lube?" he asked as he lowered me onto my bed, then smoothed his hands up my thighs to help me unhook my legs from around his waist.

"U-under my bed," I stammered.

"That's a new one," he said under his breath, and I let my head flop sideways so I could watch him crouch down and reach under my bed for the bin with my sex supplies.

I knew the moment he opened the bin, because the air got crackling hot with tension.

"You naughty boy, you said you'd only had thoughts and watched porn. But you have toys in here. Even more interesting. That blue one's almost as big as me."

Gulping, I explained weakly, "I bought them for my exes, but lately... I've used them."

Lips spreading wide in a carnivorous smile, his prominent canines looking like they were going to sink into an artery or two and claim me, he hummed.

But he left the toys there, coming onto the bed with only the lube and a condom, and then he stripped us both completely. He was almost ruthless as he manhandled me with quiet grunts.

"I'm going to wreck you," he groaned, sweeping his big hands from my lips to my ankles. He clasped my ankles and used the grip to make me bend my knees and then fold them up into my chest, leaving me completely bared to his blazing eyes and sure fingers. "So cute."

I was too out of my mind to answer, my body shivering and jumping with electric shocks as he pumped my dick, ran a thumb up the seam of my balls, then circled my hole.

"Not everyone likes anal play or sex, even if they like it alone with toys," he murmured as he snapped open the lube and squeezed some onto his fingers, "so if it doesn't feel good or you want to stop, or you need me to slow down, you better tell me, Enzo."

"Yeah, yes, okay," I promised, my voice fracturing on the last word.

When he dipped the tip of a finger inside me, I cried out so loudly. I'd never felt anything more incredible and I rolled my hips, seeking more penetration, more of that electricity.

"But some of us are just made for this," he said breathlessly as I felt his finger fill me up to the knuckle, only to start pumping at a leisurely pace right away. "Guess you're one of us."

The usage of *us* made my heart clench and ache, because it felt so right.

A sob tore out when he added another finger, more following when he found my prostate and tapped it hard and fast, circling every few beats. It was so much more fulfilling than any of the toys I'd used, his fingers hot and unyielding, and way more experienced than me.

I rose up to smash our mouths together, ecstatic and overjoyed.

His fingers were patient but relentless, and in no time, the kiss was me sobbing into his wet mouth while he rumbled, "That's it, baby, let it happen."

My mind totally disintegrated as I shot off without a hand on my dick.

It lasted so long, and I cried out weakly with one last twitch when Trentham eased his fingers out, clutching at his shoulders, begging, "Don't go, I need to suck you, I *need to*."

"Enzo," he hissed.

"Please, I need to, " I begged more, delirious and shell-shocked from the whole experience, but still so hungry and unfulfilled, which was out of this world. "Please!"

He soothed me again, helping me let go of my bent legs so I could stretch them out, moaning as I felt the ache in my ass, and pulled me down the bed. That confused me until he lay on his side facing me, his elbow digging under my pillow, which put his dick at my eye level. There were prominent veins twisting around his shaft and it curved up towards his stomach, and my mouth watered like I actually was starving for it.

Without any hesitation, I wrapped my hand around it and angled the tip onto my bottom lip, snaking my tongue over it and moaning, body jerking at the taste of him.

"Yeah," he encouraged.

I let it all go, no thoughts but *suck it, suck it* and no feelings but that great big hunger.

I slurped on his tip for a while, then changed my grip on the shaft so I could start sucking it into my mouth too, dragging up to take a quick breath before pushing down again.

Trentham's hips started making aborted thrusts and I whimpered every time because it was a demonstration that I was doing a good job, and I let go of his shaft to take handfuls of his ass.

"Shit, yeah," he shouted out as one of his hands palmed the back of my head.

I knew all I needed to do was push against his palm and he'd let me go, but I didn't want to. I wanted to stay, taking his dick as far down my throat as I could over and over until he gave it up to me.

He seemed to know it, too, because his thrusts stayed shallow but got rough, grunting every other breath until he tugged my hair and forcibly pulled my mouth off his dick.

"Too much—"

For a second I thought I'd done something wrong, but then he stroked himself once, twice, and made a noise like he was dying.

Dumbfounded, I watched spurt after spurt explode out of his dick and onto my chest and arm, so hot and viscous I felt branded by it. I realized he'd pulled me off because his load would've been too much for an amateur to swallow.

He fell onto his back, shaking the bed against the wall loudly, and laughed.

"Jetlagged now?" I guessed once he'd stopped laughing, but didn't move at all.

"Mm."

I rolled over and got up, tossing the lube into the bin

and kicking it under the bed, then got the dish towel from the kitchen to clean off my very dirty upper body and his hand.

"I think I'll need to invest in wet wipes or some hand towels," I commented as I tossed the dish towel towards my laundry hamper.

I slid the blankets out from under his big body and covered him up. I really wanted to kiss him more, tangle up our limbs and bask in this. But I knew that he wasn't looking for, or even comfortable with, affection or appreciation like that.

"Go ahead and sleep, I have to take the dogs out one last time," I told him quietly.

"How was I?" he mumbled when I was almost out of the room.

"Better than porn," I replied honestly, smiling crookedly when he just laughed sleepily.

Chapter Five

Trentham

I woke up slowly, slogging through the ends of my dreams towards alertness.

Enzo was on his stomach, head half-buried under a pillow, one leg hanging off his side of the bed, and I could feel three pet-sized lumps around my body pinning the blankets in place.

My life was solid and good, aside from the last week and whatever dumb drama I'd have to deal with becaue of Dallas for the next few months. And I had a home base in Chicago for when I wasn't on tour, a converted warehouse penthouse apartment less than a mile from Xavier's. But I couldn't ever remember waking up in bed with someone else and a bunch of pets, a scenario that would look settled and ordinary from the outside. And... it wasn't so bad.

I took a minute to soak it up before I carefully got my arms out from under the blankets and moved the Corgi aside so I could get out of the bed. The Corgi whuffed and crawled in a circle before flopping over limply, and Enzo's arm crept into my spot as if searching for me.

With a quiet snort, I went to the bathroom and then

hunted around the living room looking for my phone, turning on a lamp because Enzo had shut all the curtains last night.

I answered messages from Xavier, then screwed up my face and read Kayla's draft statement about the Dallas clusterfuck. I didn't care if people thought I'd been cheated on, but I was still pissed he hadn't had the decency to get in touch with me first. There was no way I was going to call him out on keeping up appearances after we'd broken up just so he wouldn't have any bad press before his new series premiered. I didn't want some sort of dumb feud. But it was bullshit and I needed Kayla to get in some sharp jabs so I didn't come off like an idiot.

Annoyed that I was annoyed in the first place, I grabbed my stuff and went to take a shower.

Even though there were no windows in here, I could sense it was very early in the morning, something about the air still and hushed. Something about it allowed me to take some time to simply stand under the almost-boiling water and think about last night.

It had been shocking to find all those well-loved toys under Enzo's bed, but he'd been right when he said excited didn't mean naive. While he might not have been with a man before, he hadn't had any reservations or even asked for any advice. He'd been unabashed about how he was feeling, not trying to hold off his pleasure so he could try to do it all at once.

While the blowjob hadn't had tons of skill, he hadn't tried too hard either. There had been something so refreshing about someone who wasn't out to prove how good they were. It had gotten me there faster and harder than anything else had in forever.

With a long sigh, I reached for Enzo's generic body wash and started to slip.

Cursing, I caught myself and slapped off the water because slipping in the shower was a sign that my head was in the clouds and I needed to get it on straight again.

Once I was dressed, I went to the kitchen intending to brew some coffee.

The animals were scarfing down food out of bowls in front of the dishwasher, but they looked up at me when I came close, the dogs wagging their tails and giving me canine smiles.

"Morning!" Enzo chirped from the couch, wearing flannel pants and a Downbeat tee-shirt that had the band on it, my face right over his left nipple. "You got up early."

"My sleep schedule is still all over the place."

I didn't mean to move closer, but I drifted over, leaving my suitcase next to his desk.

He had the TV on again and was flipping through new releases on one of the streaming apps. The app's suggestions for what to watch next were all fluffy sitcoms and sci-fi comedies, not a single serious drama or rated-R show or movie in the list, and I shook my head.

"Why are you looming?" he asked, then patted the couch next to him. "I'm not going to jump you or anything. Even though last night was *totally* the best. As soon as I can, I'm getting bi pride merch and updating my dating apps with the 'who I'm looking for' type information."

"I'm... glad," I managed, crossing my arms and stubbornly staying on my feet.

"It was such good luck that you needed a place to hide out, single and willing to mingle with me, so I could test out Ariane's theory that I might be into guys too," he went on happily, eyes shining as he looked up at me. "I can't wait to try out dates with men too."

Guilt would've churned because I was going to walk out in an hour or so and not see him for another however-many-years, where I would just casually give him the nod. But I caught sight of the time and frowned instead.

"Shouldn't you be getting ready to leave?"

Without looking at me, he answered, "Nope, the trip's canceled. But it's great. I still took the days off work already, so I can just chill out here and catch up on all this good stuff!"

My eyes narrowed as I demanded, "Why is it canceled?"

"Don't worry," Enzo began in an upbeat tone, eyes flicking over to the windows.

Immediately I rushed over and shoved the curtains aside.

"Welcome to Aspen?" he tried, looking guilty despite the fact that it wasn't his fault.

It was *bad.* I could barely see anything out the windows, but there was snow everywhere;so deep that only the tops of cars were above it, a couple feet of snow piled on the roofs. The air was gray and swirling with more snow, and I couldn't see any of the mountains.

"No," I said loudly, striding away from the view.

He smiled a little and shook his head. "Oh wow, can you control the weather?"

"Cra-a-ap," I moaned, pulling up my email.

There was already a message from the event's organizer waiting for me, nearly lost in the dozens of emails I got every day. I skimmed it, my heart sinking.

"My thing tonight is canceled," I told Enzo, as if he couldn't have guessed, "and they're not rescheduling *at this time* because it's not like they can push it back a night or something. Ugh, I'm going to have to get a new flight out of here tonight and go back to Chicago early."

Enzo looked up from his own phone. "The weather forecast shows we're going to get up to another eighteen inches by tomorrow morning. Skiing's going to be so great next weekend!"

He didn't say the rest, but he didn't need to.

"All flights are delayed?"

"Until tomorrow morning, at the earliest," he confirmed, kicking his feet up onto the coffee table like he didn't have a care in the world. "Whoever organized your thing is kind of an idiot, huh? Like, this is Aspen, in the middle of the Rockies, and it's the middle of winter! It might be sunny almost year-round, but we get snowstorms all the time."

I turned in a circle, at a loss. "I should pack up and just go over to the hotel."

"No way!" he exclaimed, waving his hands. "If you're stuck, then so are those paparazzi."

"But..."

A beaming, sparkly grin split his face in two and made me wince with its strength.

"Why are you down? You're on vacation too, basically. I have tons of food and beer and the heat's working. We can just hole up and watch movies or play video games."

I wanted to tell him *fuck no*. The plan had been to give him the best night of his life and then get the hell out of here this morning, leaving him smarter and me sated.

But now I couldn't leave and that smile meant he was feeling optimistic. Lucky.

Pointing a finger at him, I gave him a withering glare. "This is *not* fate, Enzo."

"Sure thing, Trentham!"

"Fuck," I mumbled, crumbling onto the couch next to him, making it shudder.

He shot me a triumphant, coy look and fluttered his eyelashes. "So what looks good?"

"I'm not watching any of that rom com shit," I shot back. "I just had to read through a statement drafted by our publicist about my quote-unquote love life. I've had enough of that for the week. Or, you know, the rest of my life. So unless you have a movie that's about getting sweet, sweet revenge on your ex, I'm not interested in anything that has to do with love, Enzo."

Clutching Slush against his chest like the dog could protect him against my anger, his eyes widened and he hastily agreed, "No, yeah, get it, one hundred percent hear you. No need to, like, rip my TV off the wall and smash it. I like other kinds of things too. You... tell me when you see something that looks... revenge-y or angry enough for you, okay?"

I grunted, but when he wiggled around a little, that niggling guilt nipped at my heels and I unbent enough to look over, though I didn't touch him. "You feeling good this morning?"

"Yeah, of course," he said, looking puzzled.

Praying for patience, I cracked my neck and tried again. "Your ass, Enzo. How's your ass?"

That made his mouth pop open before he snickered. "*That's* your idea of aftercare?"

When I scowled and snatched the remote from him, he reached out to pat my shoulder like he was consoling me for being an idiot. "My ass is good too. But I'll probably have to only eat soup and milkshakes for the next week, because my jaw and throat are super sore."

Unbelievably, I felt heat crawl up the back of my neck.

Deciding there was no good way to answer that, I puttered around the app until I saw a movie that had enough action to keep me interested and enough jokes to keep him happy.

"How about this one?" I muttered.

"You got it!" I hit play while he bounced up, calling over his shoulder, "It's officially vacation, so I'm making super buttery popcorn. Do you want some tea and bourbon too?"

Weighing my state of mind, I tossed up my hands. "Why not?"

"That's the spirit!" he exclaimed, whistling happily as he moved around the kitchen.

"Keep it light, don't break his heart when you can't fucking leave," I muttered to myself.

Chapter Six

Enzo

Sometime during our third movie and fourth... fifth...? hot toddy, the power went out.

"Whoa, what the fuck?" Trentham rumbled from next to me.

"The building has generators," I reassured him. "This happens every winter. But they don't kick in automatically and it could take a few hours for the maintenance guy to get here and get them up and running. I have a little battery-operated space heater in the bedroom."

His hand bumped into my leg and then patted around until he found my hand.

Since I knew *I* didn't need to be reassured, I figured he wasn't used to this sort of thing.

"Come on, let's go into the bedroom. You get water, I'll round up the animals."

Without saying anything else, he turned on his cell's flashlight and went for the fridge, while I whistled for the dogs and double-checked that Eloise was already in her usual spot on the carpet under my dresser.

"Slumber party," I exclaimed as Trentham joined us.

He set down the water and his suitcase, then bent to unzip it and pull out another long-sleeved thermal and sweatpants. Unceremoniously, he stripped and changed, the flashes of skin and chest hair bringing me back to last night and making my dick twitch excitedly.

But it was more than just seeing a gorgeous, naked man I'd touched last night.

It was the domesticity of the moment, getting changed into pajamas on a cold winter's night, nothing else to do but snuggle up in bed and share warmth, and talk and doze.

I shivered at the idea, at the chance that fate—yes, *fate*—had dropped into my lap like a shiny present. Spending all day on my couch, watching movies and putting lunch together, plus the slow-burn buzz of the hot toddies, had gotten my hopes up. This clinched the deal.

Trentham was gruff and he looked imposing, but there was something so much softer and caring under there, even if he'd maybe forgotten about it. His devotion to Downbeat and everyone in the band, plus their publicist and manager, was obvious in the little stories he'd told about this last tour. His honor was there in the disappointment and disgust in his voice when he'd even briefly mentioned this ex who'd gone off and gotten married with no warning.

And with every hour that had passed, he'd relaxed a little more, his mouth softening, his shoulders dropping, his hands uncurling from fists into this invitation I'd barely resisted.

'This isn't a free show," he said.

Startling, I laughed it off and turned away to turn on the space heater and grab a few extra blankets to pile onto the bed, then joined him and the dogs under the blankets.

"You know, the power going out seems like another point in favor of fate," I had to say.

He kicked my shins lightly with his sock-covered feet. "It's not fate, it's winter in Aspen, you said so yourself. You're not saying you lied to me earlier, are you?"

"Ooh, so big and scary," I teased, poking one of his shoulders. "Come on, there's nothing to do until the generators kick in but talk, have sex, or sleep, and I'm definitely not tired yet."

"I'd rather have sex than talk."

"Great endorsement for sex: it's better than talking."

I'd been so good all day, respecting his blunt, direct warning last night that it had been strictly a one-time, special circumstances thing. It hadn't been difficult because I enjoyed his massively snide commentary on the movies, which had gotten funnier with each drink.

But now we were literally huddled together for warmth, and I laughed while edging closer, knowing it wasn't subtle but I didn't care because he hadn't stopped me yet.

"You felt it too last night, didn't you? I've never felt chemistry like that before. I don't want to waste this chance to explore it some more." When I had burrowed all the way against his body, I whispered, "Unless you don't want to. I can just close my eyes and pretend this is..."

My breath whooshed out of me when he snaked his arms around me and squeezed.

"Yeah, I'm here a second night and we didn't expect it," he murmured into my hair. "And yeah, last night was fun and sexy for me too. This is the first time I've held still with anyone other than the Downbeat family in a really long time. I didn't know how much I needed it."

I started to tell him I was glad, not just because I'd thought he would go stir crazy after one movie, but because I felt pretty special that he was able to unwind with me.

He kept going, though, and it came out rough. "*But.* We

can spend time under all these blankets having more sex. But it's not fate, okay? I'm still heading out once I can get a flight."

For some reason, I tried to jerk out of his hold at the way he'd said that.

"Hey, hey," he soothed.

I shoved my hands into his meaty chest and broke his hold.

"You seem to be confused," I told him as firmly as I could. "I'm a happy person who believes in love and listening when the universe is giving me chances to be even happier. I'm not a dumbass who thinks sex always, or always has to, mean anything more than fun pleasure. I'd rather sleep than listen to your condescending lecturing."

"*Damnit.*"

"What? Are you going to try to convince me that isn't what you meant now?" I snapped.

"Enzo," he snapped back before his fingers gripped my face and he rolled me onto my back, looming over me nearly invisible. "People who want to sleep with me—or hang out with me or be my friend, if I'm honest—want to sleep with Trentham-from-Downbeat. Not *me*. And that's fine with me, because I've got all the friends I need and I'm not looking for love. This has been... really nice. But I know you. Your brother is my best friend. I don't want to hurt you."

I made a *pfffft* noise. "Whether I get hurt or not is my responsibility, not yours."

"But I still don't want it to happen," he argued, his frustration clear in his voice.

"Only because I'm Xav's younger bro—"

I cut myself off to gasp and point an accusatory finger in his face.

"Ohh my God, it's not that I'm his brother," I cried, "it's that I'm his *much younger* brother. You think I'm like a baby duckling who's going to imprint on the first guy I get with, never mind the ten women before him?"

Trentham groaned and dropped his forehead on mine, his fingers stroking the soft underside of my jaw. "You're imagining my thoughts and then twisting them up," he argued gruffly. "But I really appreciate you reminding me that you're fourteen years younger than me."

Despite the words, his body softened against mine until I could feel his half-hard dick drop onto my inner thigh.

"I'm way more of an adult than you are," I whispered, grabbing his thick waist and slowly working my hands down towards his ass. "I own this place, I have a full-time job with benefits, and I've been in committed, loving relationships. Whereas you're still allergic to love like an eighteen-year-old dipshit, and I bet you don't know how to pay your mortgage, schedule a doctor's appointment, pay taxes, grocery shop, or log into your own bank account."

By the end of my short rant, he was shaking with laughter, which made my dick finish filling up because it felt so good. I loved having soft, laughter-filled sex.

"Touché," he finally chuckled.

"Kiss me," I told him.

He sighed and suddenly rolled us over, blankets dragging heavily and tangling us up, and the dogs yipped in outrage and scrambled out and off the bed.

"Ohh, that's a neat trick," I breathed.

As his legs fell open to give me space between them, our erections rubbed together through the layers of clothes. I wanted more, so I struggled to sit up, perched between his thighs, and flung off the blankets so they wouldn't strangle us and stop us from moving.

He smoothed his hands up under my shirt, my glasses getting caught in it as he took it off. I swore and fished them out. Once they were safely on the nightstand, I tugged up on his shoulders so he curled up enough to take his thermal off too. I moaned in pleasure when our torsos pressed hot and eager together, his chest hair scratching my skin and lighting it up.

Rocking his hips up into mine, he licked into my mouth, one hand tunneling through my messy hair to direct my head where he wanted. We made out like that until the heat kicked on with a loud click and blast of hot air.

I raised my head up to say, "That was fast."

"Now we can take off the rest of our clothes without shriveling up," he replied practically, already tugging down my pajamas and boxers.

I fell sideways unexpectedly from the force of his moves, laughing when my dick popped free and smacked my stomach.

The humor died out when he stripped off his bottoms, displaying his sexy body again. My hands went to his stomach, watching its muscles flex and curve into my touch.

"We should try something new tonight," he suggested.

"Like what?" I asked, my mind going fuzzy from how raspy and shot his voice was.

Interlacing our fingers, he guided me past his dick, lower down to his hole.

Shooting my head up, I gaped at him. "You—?"

"Yeah, baby," he confirmed, his eyes heavy-lidded but hot on me. "I told you, some of us have asses made for this. Why don't you stretch me out and put that pretty cock in me?"

"Dirty talk," I squeaked, my fingers flexing involuntarily against him.

Snorting lightly, he shook his head and asked, "Do you want me?"

Dumbstruck, I nodded mutely, because that was the silliest question ever. Hadn't I made it abundantly clear that I wanted him, last night and tonight? Hadn't I made the first moves?

He hummed, the low note sounding patient but pleased, and relaxed back onto the pillows, one hand moving to play with the head of his dick. "Or you can sit there and watch."

That got me moving, diving my upper body off the bed to reach the bin, digging blindly until I felt the lube, knowing the unused condom from last night was still on my nightstand. Levering myself back up, I caught him staring at my ass unabashedly, and I grinned and arched it up a little bit, then pushed up onto all fours before turning around to face him again.

A gentler kind of smile shaped his kiss-swollen lips and I paused to smile helplessly back at him, before he nudged me with a knee and got me moving again. I ducked my head and got comfortable between his legs, which he bent up, but kept his feet flat on the mattress.

Putting lube on my fingers, I used my dry hand to cup one of his ass cheeks and spread it to give me the space to play over him. I'd always been soft and thorough during foreplay, but sort of disconnected from it, since it was more practical than romantic, just a necessary prelude to lovemaking.

But Trentham wasn't acting like this was strictly foreplay, tossing his head back and grabbing his own hair as his mouth fell open in bliss.

I realized this must be what I'd looked like last night, losing my mind on two of his fingers.

"Give me more," he demanded in a guttural voice, spreading his legs wider.

I obliged, then watched in amazement at how easily his body opened up to take me in. Following the rhythm of his rolling hips intently, I was lost in it until he jerked and his dick twitched in the air above his stomach like he was about to come, and he moaned.

"Baby, now."

It was hard to pull my fingers out and leave him empty, even temporarily, so I could put on the condom and grip the base of my dick to help guide it into him.

But it was worth it when his upper body arched sharply upwards, sinking his ass down onto my dick completely in one heartbeat. He was hot as hell around me, tight and rippling with every slow thrust I made, his jaw clenched and the same little grunts he'd made while I was sucking him tearing out of him.

Pride and awe and that sense of rightness I'd felt last night washed over me, swallowing me up and protecting me against anything but this, no future, no past, no pain, only pleasure.

I moaned and sighed, my thighs and stomach burning a little from the slightly different set of muscles it took to make love to his ass, and it only heightened the new experience.

"*Uhn*," he shouted, and his big body twisted like a flame in the wind, chasing something, using me. Bringing me such pleasure and joy in turn, so willing to give him something he wanted. "Faster, fucking faster, Enzo," he demanded, one hand grabbing his dick roughly.

I put my back into it, hooking his heavy legs over my elbows and using them as leverage.

He seized up until the only part of him moving was his

arm, almost vibrating over the head of his dick. It was so beautiful, watching him and watching myself impale him to the hilt, and when his face collapsed in agony with a ragged gasp, I came instantly right with him.

If I'd thought last night's orgasm was long, this one was infinite, a frozen moment in time where my heart flooded with every great emotion and then flooded the condom too.

When we were spent, I slid one arm under his lower back, keeping him pinned onto me as I carefully arched over him for a kiss. I thought that he might reject it, turn his head enough that the kiss would land on his cheek, but he let catch his open mouth in a soft kiss.

The kisses went on and on, my dick slipping out some- time and making him whimper and press closer, as if he needed to still be able to feel it even if it wasn't inside him anymore.

"I have to wash up," he murmured eventually, then smoothed his hands up my back and kissed me once, twice more, as if he couldn't imagine leaving the bed without them first.

Chapter Seven

Trentham

My whole body was like jelly as I made my way out of Enzo's bed and into the bathroom next door, actually putting my hand on the wall to brace myself and stay upright.

My *mind* was like jelly too, actually, oozing out my ears and leaving me dumb.

When I'd suggested that he fuck me, I expected something... coltish. A newborn horse finding its legs, shaky and uncoordinated. But I should've known better, because he'd blasted aside my expectations with his kissing skills too. There had been nothing self-conscious or unsure in how he'd prepped me or how he'd matched my movements once he was inside me. Desire and satisfaction had carried me away, had let me kiss him endlessly in the aftermath.

I will never underestimate people again, I thought with a snort as I finished up and staggered back to his bedroom, turning off the space heater on my way back into his bed.

Sprawling out spread-eagle next to Enzo, I groaned and stretched my muscles.

"It's only eight-thirty," he said, his voice a little rougher than usual. "I'm going to go make some sandwiches and grab some chips. Do you need to doze off and recover?"

"Very funny," I said, sitting up again. "I'll come sit with you."

I didn't know why I'd offered, when I shouldn't encourage familiarity. But Enzo was so warm and undemanding, and I was damn tired after the tour. So we both put clothes back on and then I trailed after him into the kitchen, where I straddled one of the chairs backward.

"Now that we had sex, and I'm wide awake and you claim you don't need to doze," he said with cheerful casualness as he gathered up bread, ham and swiss, and mustard, "the only thing left to do is talk, Trentham. You' have to tell me everything, or I'll snuggle you all night."

It was preposterous, but it made me laugh anyway. "Is that right?"

"I know why I'm happy. I don't know who, or what, made you so cynical," he reasoned. "We have a lot of time to kill tonight and my laptop is dead. I'm not wasting my cell battery; it's dangerous when there's bad weather like this, especially if the phone lines get knocked out."

I folded my forearms on the back of the chair and rested my chin on top of them. He moved lightly, like a dancer or a fencer maybe, heavy-handed with the mustard and how thick he sliced the bread, but his cheeks were flushed still from the bedroom and I couldn't resist.

"It's short, but it's definitely not sweet. You sure you want to know?"

He glanced over at me, and the set of his lips was familiar, some genetic quirk he shared with Xavier and their mother. "Happy doesn't mean nothing bad has ever happened to me."

Grunting because I was pretty sure I would've known if something really bad had ever happened to him, I said, "When I came out to my parents, they told me I wasn't their son."

Enzo stopped moving, chips tumbling out of the upended bag and landing on one of the sandwiches. His throat worked and then he looked squarely at me and said, "I'm so sorry, Becker. I'll just never understand how people can be so cruel, and parents... It's not right."

"To them, it's a sin, and never mind they sin plenty themselves," I said quietly, standing up and gently taking the chip bag out of his hand and taking over with the food.

"They weren't like your parents before that anyway. They judged everything. Who did I think I was, pretending I was better than everyone else, getting straight A's and refusing to play football? Leaving Tennessee for New York City, gambling for a living and hanging out with hooligans? It got to be too much, being silent about all that and hiding who I was, too. Jorge took me in, let me break down and then get back up again. Downbeat is my only family."

By the time I was done, he was shaking beside me.

I leaned in and gave him a simple kiss, right at the corner of his taut mouth. "It's okay, baby, it was almost twenty years ago."

"It's *not* okay," he whispered, "I'm so upset I made you tell me."

"You can't make me do anything," I told him, leading him to the table before I brought over the food and bottled water. "Anyway, I'm not cynical. I know what Gin and Kayla have is true love. I know what Seth found with Astrid is true love. The way they describe being in love, that's how I love my best friends, just minus the sexual and romantic feelings. I've connected with people I date, I'm not heartless. But I just... never loved anyone romantically like that."

The more I spoke, the more he seemed to come back to himself, but he still didn't look happy, which he confirmed when he asked, "Would you describe yourself as aromantic then?"

"I suppose that's a fair question," I said slowly. "But it's a chicken or the egg situation. I'm almost forty and I've slept with and dated a lot of people, Enzo. Some of them put butterflies in my chest or hearts in my eyes or took my breath away. But none of those feelings lasted more than a moment or two, really. At some point, I stopped looking for that. So which is it, am I incapable of romantic feelings, or have I just not met a single person I could fall in love with?"

He winced at that, and I felt guilty about causing it, but I wouldn't lie to him.

"But you sing love songs," he whispered, staring down at his bottle of water.

It was beside the point that I didn't write them, or that Xavier sang and I played guitar.

I wanted to move away from things that made him sad. Or... sad for me, or sad on my behalf. So I refocused the conversation using a cheap trick. "Do you have any dessert?"

"Dessert?"

"Yeah, you know, cookies, banana bread, donuts," I prompted, looking around at his countertops, which only had a knife block, a bowl of fruit, and then all the weird shit kitchens seemed to collect like pizza coupons, a power cord, and a lopsided pyramid of coins.

"I was planning to leave on vacation today," he said apologetically, "so I ate all the good and perishable stuff already. There's nothing worse than coming home to a smelly place."

I grinned and commented, "Another example of how you and Xavier are different."

"He's focused on creative things," he said loyally. "It is lucky he's good at it—lucky you're all so good at it—so he can afford a cleaning service. If not, he'd live like Oscar the Grouch."

"Do you remember him when he was a kid?"

Pushing aside his plate, Enzo leaned in and propped one hand on his palm. "Not really; in my earliest memories he was already in college."

He stretched out his other hand and played with my hair. I was going to have to change the cut soon, since my hairline was pulling back above my temples—or not, I thought as his fingers pushed my hair back and trailed over my hairline, smiling softly.

"All of the photos and family videos from when he was a kid are at my parent's house though. Mom and Aunt Sylvie set off the fire alarm at Xav's dad's auto shop sometime after the divorce, then broke into his place and stole everything he'd kept, the jerk."

The words stroked over me, and I leaned into his delicate, questing touch, wondering when anyone had last been this curious and sweet with me, in or out of bed.

"You don't need to see them, though. Five or thirty-five, Xav's the same. Charming, maybe not the sharpest tool in the shed, with an incredible voice," he summed up, sounding wistful.

I tilted my head and reached out to run my thumb over his chin and bottom lip.

"You know he has his insecurities too, baby," I said, my voice hushed in this little bubble of peace and timelessness between us, sitting at his kitchen table with snow piled up outside to keep us here. "He feels like he always has to be *on* for people to like him, or love him. I'm not the charming one, I'm the edgy, intimidating one, but I feel that too, people's expectations."

"I'm not sure I really know him—or you," Enzo admitted, his hand falling away, and I felt the loss like something sharp in my guts, like I was missing something I'd only just gotten.

I pushed the feeling aside, hoping that I could at least help him understand his brother a little better, since their relationship would last forever, while ours wouldn't. "We've had so many great times, so many great stories, and it's a lucky life we live, for sure. But people don't... want to stick around during the downtimes when we really need it, need quiet and no pressure, when we can say what we want and not worry it'll end up online and stuff. People want to be with Downbeat's frontman, they want the VIP passes and to go to awards shows."

His face scrunched up a little, as if that didn't make any sense to him, and God, did that hit me hard. He hadn't once asked me to tell him wild stories or ask what any of the other famous people I knew were like or if I'd slept with them. All he'd asked about was... *me*.

"Is-is that what happened with Dallas?"

I exhaled hard and shrugged uncomfortably, sitting back too so we weren't touching.

"We were introduced a few years ago. He's pouty and self-centered, but on our first date, we had a really interesting conversion about queer representation in Hollywood. It was a good fit for both of us; he had a really busy shooting schedule and I was about to head back into the studio. I felt like we were looking for similar things and it was low-pressure. But he got noticed for that role and it led to bigger parts, which is good for him, right? Except I started to feel more like arm candy, a punkish accessory who looked great standing next to him on red carpets."

"I'm sure that wasn't true."

The stubborn optimism made me smile ruefully.

"The last straw was him losing his shit because I dared to have a concert the night of a premiere. I *just had to* be there. It was clear he didn't care if he saw me or spent time together afterwards. I ended it, but he was up for this part and cried about how someone had said he wasn't reliable, we couldn't break up and reinforce that. And then it was another thing, and another. I haven't talked to him directly in months. We play coy—you know, he posts a pic on Instagram of him looking forlorn in front of an L.A. sunset, tags me, then a few hours later I post a selfie looking lonely after a show with London behind me, tagging him. It's whatever."

"It is not whatever!" he denied, eyes flashing, and then suddenly he was climbing onto my lap and clasping my neck, staring at me intently eye-to-eye. "I would never do that to someone, whether they were my friend, m-my boyfriend, or my soulmate. Of course you have to ask for help sometimes, and sometimes it's selfish, but to *never* show appreciation or try to repay the favor...? That's just disrespectful, Becker. Maybe you've been famous so long, you forgot that you're so much more important than your persona or your cool rock n roll lifestyle."

Stunned by his sincerity and fierceness, I took his mouth hard and hot.

I didn't know how else to respond—it seemed stupid beyond words to mumble *thank you*. So I tried to show him I appreciated that more than I could say, without having to tell him it had been... never, if I were honest, since someone had said anything like that to me.

Pinning him between me and the table, winding my arms around his torso like a boa, I loved how his chest heaved when our lips parted to breathe.

I whined when he writhed and buried my mouth in his neck.

"If this," I muttered into his neck, debating what word to use before I went on, "chemistry is good for you, if you liked what we've done in bed, then you deserve it too. Loving someone doesn't have to be only about hearts and flowers and exclude getting down and dirty."

"I—" His breath hitched and he shook his head, his chin brushing my cheekbone with every shake. "It's never been like this before for me, Becker. I don't know... I don't know why."

I know why.

The thought rang heavy and inescapable through my mind.

Enzo wasn't the kind of person who held back or was uncomfortable with what he wanted. That was undeniable from the ridiculous—but charming, damn it—way he'd thrown himself into testing his theory that men would do something for him that women never had. But if I'd been just some guy, then the sex would've been indistinguishable from all the sex he'd had before me: supposedly about emotional connection, tepid, no *need*, no *fire*.

And I wasn't the kind of person who lied to myself or hid who I was, either. Up until now, I'd never felt like this, either, not when I'd been hoping to and not when I'd been hoping *not* to.

I hadn't lied about anything. But what was going on here...

This went way beyond sexual compatibility and hot, mutually beneficial sex. Way beyond him confirming he was into men and me blowing off steam from all the stress of the long tour and Dallas's wedding reveal fiasco.

"Baby," I rasped out, sweating, my heart trying to pound out of my chest, "yes you do."

Chapter Eight

Enzo

I went rigid with fear in Becker's hold, sure that he was about to tell me that I was feeling the triumph and thrill of figuring out that I was super damn sexually attracted to men. That my brain and body was flooded with hormones or pheromones or whatever because of that discovery and that it was cool for me, but it had been nothing but a cute diversion for him.

"I-I do?" I asked, trying to delay that heartbreak for another few seconds at least.

His dark blue eyes were zoomed in on me and hawklike, his eyebrows lowered and scrunched a little menacingly. But his mouth was lush and soft and his thumbs were sweeping soothing arcs over my lower back. Just being able to see his persona peeled back enough to see a little bit of the tired, slightly lost, wonderfully sweet man made me ache.

"This is..." He faltered, his eyes darting away from mine and all over the place like a hummingbird, but I waited, afraid if I jumped the gun, he'd just run. "This is... *real*, Enzo."

The words were vulnerable, but it took strength to get them out, despite this not being what he wanted or had been looking for when he knocked on my door less than two days ago.

"But," he continued, wincing like he hated it, and I couldn't hold back a little whine of distress. "This is also reality, and our lives are very different. I warned you. I'm based out of Chicago and I'm due to be there for awhile, but after that, it's back on the road, always gone."

My heart was racing so fast, and he'd just hit me with a one-two combination so I couldn't think at all, my mind whirling and the ground dipping and tilting under me. One hit: he felt this magical, new thing, too. Second hit: he had his own life and mine didn't fit into it.

Thumb brushing my bottom lip again, he sighed slow and sad. "I know you have a positive outlook, so I know you're thinking about all of the things we could try."

"What are you going to be doing in Chicago?" I burst out when he paused.

"Decompressing. In maybe six months, we'll be back in the studio to record," he explained. "The timeline is fuzzy there because a lot of it depends on Xavier and any other songwriters. I'm not part of that, other than telling stories to provide inspiration. Then all the ramp-up to the new album release, the interviews and radio shows, the social media. The release, with a party or concert and more press, hope-fully fun but always jam-packed. Then a tour, we like to do the U.S. first, then Asia, then Latin America, then Europe and Africa."

I probably could have pieced all of that together myself, except I usually sort of tuned Xavier out when he gave a monologue about his writing-to-touring cycle with Downbeat.

There was still something in it that I could work with, though. "Decompressing?"

He started to smile and then caught himself. "It's my homework, basically."

I grinned and fluttered my eyelashes at him, then laughed in elation when he shoved the chair under us out from the table and then carried me back into the bedroom, tossing me down into the wreckage of our earlier lovemaking. He came down next to me, lacing his fingers under his head and turning to meet my eyes over the impressive swell of his triceps.

"So you spend six months catching up on sleep, eating tacos with your friends, maybe trying to get back in peak shape or buy a new car or guitar. Play the new video games and watch the new movies or TV seasons that came out while you were on tour. That sort of thing?"

Narrowing his eyes at me almost playfully, he said with exaggerated dignity, "Exactly."

I raised my eyebrows and readjusted my pillows so I was reclining comfortably, crossing my legs at the ankles. "That's really important to your mental health, and it sounds like being Chicago is crucial to your very *survival*," I told him in the most serious tone I could manage.

"My guitars are in Chicago," he said, trying to sound offended.

My grin wobbled and slid off my face as I knotted my hands in my lap and suggested really quietly, "You could decompress here. I know it's not a super hip warehouse converted into a bachelor pad with tons of guitars mounted on the walls in the middle of Chicago, but—"

"I don't know," Trentham admitted once I'd run out of bravery.

Keeping my eyes on my lap, I nodded, feeling miserable.

"I'm not very good at doing nothing. It's part of why my place is in the middle of Chicago. I can go to my favorite club, hear music and dance. I can hang out with Downbeat people and hit up record shops. I can go to baseball games and football games. I can keep busy."

Aspen wasn't like that. It had great skiing and hiking right here, and plenty of amazing places to visit within three hours by car. I loved it, had grown up here and thrived here. But I kept busy with my job, plus day hikes, weekends camping, and skiing with my friends.

"If I were here," he concluded, "I'd just be in your hair all the time. And the press would figure out I was here real quick, and they'd bug you all the time too. I don't want that for you."

The apologetic, gentle tone made me angry, and I jumped off the bed and paced around my bedroom, almost tripping over Eloise when she wound between my feet like a ninja.

"Enzo—"

"No!" I cut him off. "Sounds like you already know what you're going to do. So what was the point of making me say how I feel? What was the point of, of kissing me like... *that?*"

All the muscles in his big, beefy body bunched up and he closed his eyes tight.

"I didn't want to leave it unsaid. I never want you to think that what you were feeling was silly or one-sided. Or to think *I* think it's silly. And..." His ribs expanded so much his shirt rode up an inch or two, showing off his hairy lower stomach. "And this is new for me too and who else am I going to talk to about this, other than the person who's in it with me?"

"But I don't have any answers," I exploded, my chest

seizing up, making it hard for me to breathe. My voice wobbled when I kept going. "This is a small life, but it's all I want. I don't want to quit my job and trail after you like some panting clinger. I don't want you to feel cooped up and trapped and bored here, then run off in relief when it's time to record. And I'm too affectionate and too much of a homebody for long-distance to keep me satisfied."

Defeated, I crumpled onto the bed again, burrowing my face into Becker's chest, desperately relieved and desperately sad when his arms came around me immediately.

"I'm sorry, baby," he confessed roughly sometime later.

Hating to hear it, because I knew it was final, knew it was the start of an ending when our beginning had barely begun, I rolled away from him and curled up into a ball.

I wasn't ashamed of the tears welling up—like I'd told him, I made my own choices and if I got hurt, it was my responsibility to handle it, not his responsibility to save me from it.

But when he eased up behind me, sliding an arm under my pillows and carefully wrapping the other arm around my ribs so his hand covered the base of my throat, I let go. The tears came fast and silent, but my body was shaking and my breathing was loud and erratic, so he had to know what was happening. He just pressed in closer, hard and soft all at once, protective even if he was trying to protect me from himself, and kissed the back of my neck.

"You've given me such a gift, Enzo," he whispered between kisses. "I'll never forget it."

"Me either," I cried.

We might not forget it, we might value it, but I knew we'd never be like this again.

· · ·

When Bruiser shoved his cold nose in my ear and woke me up early the next morning, I dragged myself out of bed to walk the dogs and then feed them and Eloise on autopilot.

Becker came into the kitchen while I was staring at my phone, reading that the weather had cleared up. My heartbeat was erratic because I knew the end was coming any second.

"Hey," Becker said, his voice rough and tight. "I, uh…"

"Booked your flight," I finished without looking up at him. "When is it?"

He came into my line of sight, and it was too far away and too close all at once. "Seven."

I nodded and tucked my phone in my pocket, then my hands hung limp at my sides.

"I'll go now," he said, and there was something so defeated about it that I finally looked up at him. The toll of last night was visible on his face and it might've made me feel relieved, except I never wanted to hurt him or add fuel to his cynical outlook. "That way you can…"

"What was the first guitar you bought?" I blurted out.

"A Fender Strat," he answered slowly. "Why?"

With a gulp, I said, "You don't have to leave now. I'm not ready for you to leave yet. Promise I won't try to change your mind about anything. But just… give me more time."

I tried not to react when he smiled at me, a sweet, almost *shy* thing. Like he couldn't believe me, but he wasn't going to ask if I was sure in case I changed my mind.

We ate cereal plain because I didn't have any milk left, and for a few minutes, the loud crunches were the only noises we made. I had a million things I wanted to know about him, but I wasn't sure I should ask. How would I ever be casual or cool when we inevitably met again? He and Xavier would always be best friends, and Xavier had been bothering me about going to Chicago or meeting the band wherever they had shows in places I wanted to see.

But I shoved those problems aside to deal with another day. This time with him was a gift, and I shouldn't waste it because it would suck to see Becker again someday.

"Do you want to take a walk?" I asked. "The dogs haven't gotten as much exercise as they like the last couple days. If you wear a hat and scarf, no one will be able to recognize you."

"I'd like that." He studied me for a long moment, heat flashing in his eyes for a split second before he stomped it out. "I'll have to borrow a scarf from you though."

Grinning, I jumped up and said, "Great! Let's gear up and go."

It was awkward getting ready, each of us trying not to look at the other when we changed out of pajamas. But once we were outside, the dogs going crazy sniffing the snow and peeing every ten feet, I breathed in the alpine winter air and felt my nerves settle. Becker seemed to relax once he was outside too, like maybe it felt like the right size to fit his giant body.

"So tell me about this first Fender Strat," I prompted after we'd gotten out of my neighborhood and were on a trail that ran along the edge of the trees. "Was it new?"

"God, no, it was in terrible shape," he answered with a low rumbly chuckle.

We walked and talked for what felt like hours, Becker eventually picking up the dogs and carrying them once they were lagging as far behind us as their leashes allowed. My nose was numb and we used up all the tissues I had in the travel pack I kept in my coat.

But the conversation flowed between us and it was so wonderful, I felt like I was walking on air. Nothing could take these memories away from me, and nothing could ever make me regret getting to know him so well. Not even the sadness that crept in later weakened my certainty, once we were on the couch, wrapped in blankets to thaw out after the long walk.

By the time Becker couldn't delay packing any more, we were both losing our voices and the stretches of quiet between speaking had gotten longer. I wanted to trail after him, but made myself stay on the couch, taking off my glasses and scrubbing my eyes.

"Okay," he rasped out when he came back, suitcase in hand, boots already on.

I stood up and shifted from foot to foot. I wanted to hug him, to say we should keep in touch even though I knew it was a terrible idea because I'd never be able to move on. He wouldn't agree anyhow, not wanting to give false hope that anything else would happen.

But I didn't want to cry or make him worry about me.

So I adjusted my glasses and walked to the door. "Thanks for... everything, Becker."

He cleared his throat, then darted in to kiss my cheek before shuffling back. "Bye, baby."

Chapter Nine

Trentham

March in Chicago could kiss my ass. It was really cold and windy. And it was *sleeting*, which was just the diarrhea of precipitation. If I were headed somewhere fun, it would be manageable, but I was going to a radio show where our goal was *to tease the upcoming album*, according to Kayla's strict instructions. My plan was to keep my mouth shut, because I hadn't felt like teasing or being communicative or friendly or *anything* the slightest bit positive.

At least not since I'd walked away from Enzo three months ago, my chest cracked open like I was about to have fucking open heart surgery. I might as well have torn it out myself and left the ragged, air-deprived thing on his bed, for all the good it had done me since then.

Yeah, my decompressing had been going *super* well.

I stomped into the radio station and found Xavier, who hollered with loathsome cheer when he spotted me, "Hey, Trentham! I'm so ready to tease Chicagoland this morning."

"You're hilarious," I mumbled.

We'd done countless radio interviews over the years but

we appeared on this show much more regularly than some others, since they were local. So it wasn't a big deal and I zoned out. Xavier was the one they really wanted anyhow, since he was actually hilarious.

"...visited my baby bro in Aspen last month," Xavier finished some story, the deejays laughing while the mention of Enzo had my guts clenching, but I tried to ignore them.

"And what about you, Trentham?" one of the deejays asked. "Done anything fun?"

My mind was completely blank.

"Dudes, Wrecker hasn't been fun since Dallas got married," Xavier told them.

There was no way in hell I'd said a word about the thing with Enzo to him. He'd kill me.

He'd known there was something wrong this whole time, but I should've known he thought it was the nightmarish shit with Dallas's surprise wedding. Except after Aspen, I hadn't wanted to ever think about Dallas again. I'd let Kayla handle the whole thing like the pro she was, without having to mop up after me when I inevitably fucked up.

"Stop calling me that," I growled, snapping back to the here and now.

"Just as soon as you stop being Wrecker Becker, smashing everyone's good moods with your epic scowls and total inability to give a crap," he baited me.

Xavier was family and had been for damn near twenty years, but I just *couldn't* talk to him about this. Definitely not when he was cornering me like this while we were live on-air.

Digging deep for a sense of humor, I grinned at the deejays and winked at them. "I couldn't be happier for

Dallas, I hear he had a great death scene on—what was it called?"

"Ouch," one of the deejays laughed. "So what's up? Why are you so mean to Xavier?"

"I'm a complex man, guys. But Xavier, he's the voice. So I let him do his thing."

Xavier gasped and kicked my ankle. "*Let me!*"

"Guess we're doing couples' counseling today," the other deejay joked. "Xavier, tell Trentham how you feel about that. Wait a second though, we have to get that bleep ready to go, because we know how much you like to use words that we'd definitely get fined for letting air."

Never able to resist a good mood for long, just like his brother, Xavier gave up for the time being and laughed at the deejay. "You got me, I love all the bad words. But seriously, I'm just giving Trentham a hard time here because I love the face he makes—yeah, that one!" he crowed when I glared at him. "He's got the scowl, and I've got the soul!"

"The scowl and the soul, that would be a great album title," I said.

"Someone write that down," Xavier shouted excitedly, almost loud enough to shatter all the glass in the booth. "Now how about I tell you the title of our *current* new album and then give you the inside scoop on where it came from and what it's all about?"

They carried on and I zoned out again, until we were walking out and Xavier *tripped me*. I crashed into a door that swung open, and I swore a blue streak as I tried to catch myself.

"Seriously, what the fuck is wrong with you?" Xavier demanded without an ounce of guilt while I breathed raggedly and pushed myself off the door, finding us in a bathroom.

I lunged around him, shaking off his hand violently when he tried to stop me.

"Becker."

The sound of my first name stopped me cold.

"You outmaneuvered me back there, but this is total crap," he told me, slumping back against the paper towel dispenser and looking worried. "So, here we are, in a place to get rid of crap, and you're going to talk. I wasn't lying back there, you've been in a funk since Dallas."

It wasn't the first time he'd pried and dug, but I couldn't give in because I wasn't going to half-ass explain it, which felt the same as lying. It was why I'd been avoiding him as much as possible, but I wouldn't let the band down too by canceling the appearance.

"Just leave it, Xav. You're not going to want to hear it," I threatened him seriously.

He dug his fingers into his hair and corkscrewed them. "The only thing that's happened to you anytime recently was Dallas getting married, dude. What else could it be?"

"Not a fucking chance I'm in a dark mood because of Dallas, man," I scoffed. "I already explained we were only keeping up appearances for his reputation, so it was just a PR hassle when he got married. I haven't been in a crappy mood because of him."

There must have been something about the way I emphasized *him*, because Xavier was all over that shit. "So something else happened? With some*one* else? Just tell me, please."

My chest started heaving and I kept shaking my head, no idea how to explain.

Xavier clapped his hands on my shoulders, a steady pressure through the wool of my coat, and bared his teeth in a fierce, taunting grin. "Let's sweat blood, Trentham. Hit me."

But all I could do was gasp out helplessly, too frayed to hold it in anymore, "*Enzo.*"

For a few seconds, Xavier made a generic *what the hell are you saying* face. But as he connected the dots, and his cheeks went red and his eyes got as big as basketballs.

I thought he was going to blow a gasket, but he shouted, "*Gin owes me a hundred bucks!*"

"*What?*" I roared back at him, even though I wasn't really a big yeller at all.

"I *swore* you'd fallen in love and then run away because you're a giant *idiot* when it comes to your own feelings!" He jumped up and down, using my shoulders to go higher, his smile so pure and huge, it not only reminded me of Enzo's, it confused the crap out of me. "Gin told me no way, so I bet her a hundred bucks you're totally in love for the first time in your whole life!"

Suddenly I crushed him against me, making him wheeze. "That's all you have to say?"

"You're my family, Trentham," he reminded me, wiggling his arms free to scrub over my hair. "You think I'd ever even agree to ask if you could crash at Enzo's if I didn't trust you?"

"This is a *lot* more than crashing at his place."

Xavier pretended to gag, shoving me back and waving his hands. "Dude, no details. *Ever.*" But then his expression morphed into determined and serious. "I know you. So let me help you out, since you clearly can't work this out on your own. You're miserable here. Go to Aspen."

I smacked my forehead and drove my hand through my hair. "We went over this, Xav. I didn't just cut and run without talking to him. He's got a job and friends, and I need to keep busy. We'll be in the studio pretty soon, and then it's all zero to sixty, traveling all the time."

He leveled me with a look, one that he didn't unleash very often. It was the look that said he'd known me for a very long time, knew all my history and my baggage. "That's not the real problem and you know it. You're freaked out. You felt something and you don't know how to deal. So you made up some bullshit about how it wouldn't work, so why try at all?"

My first reaction was a snarl, but it petered out.

"My brother is happy and so fucking sweet, Beck," he said. "It's easy to write him off as young and naive, and to think he doesn't know what the hell he wants. He told me he had gotten some advice that peeled his eyes open to a new, or emerging, part of himself with men."

"It's not that," I argued immediately. "It could have been that, but I knew it wasn't."

"Admit it, you've been with people that only kind of caught your attention because we've been working so fucking hard for years, forming the band, figuring out our sound, learning how to grow and be recognized. It didn't leave much time for any of us to really hone in on anything else. I always felt like it was crazy greedy to want this amazing life we have with Downbeat *and* to even hope for some soulmate, or soulmates in my case, to love like crazy too."

I cracked an out of practice smile and agreed, "Yeah. It wasn't a priority."

"Well, the universe doesn't give a shit about priorities, and things change, man. We evolve and just when we start to get cocky with how well it's going for us, bam. Something comes at us and knocks us right off our tower and onto our asses. You can't run from it."

"That was a good speech." I rocked back on my heels and sighed. "I do... want it all."

"Fuck yeah," he cheered, and then danced around, wrestling his cell out of his skin-tight pants so he could tap madly until it rang on speaker. "Gin!" he said to our drummer. "No time for jokes. Trentham is in love with Enzo and he should go be with him. Any problems?"

"No—damn it, I owe you money. Ugh. But you know what, I'm not even mad. Trentham, you there?" I grunted and she laughed. "Life's an adventure, and love's the best. Chicago's just our home base, but we can make music and give interviews and all that shit anywhere. I love flying; I like Colorado. We can snowboard and get our freak on in national parks. Separately."

My lips parted, arguments at the ready, but I knew they were all hollow and fake.

"I'll message everyone and we'll meet at my place, like, right now," Xavier announced.

He dragged me out of the bathroom and all the way to his place, where the others showed up only a few minutes later, and I admitted what had been going on with me.

Xavier took over, running through our options for how we could make it all work.

I knew it was massively premature—I hadn't talked to Enzo in months, had no idea if he'd even want to see me ever again, let alone want it all too—but I let them do this.

My voice was gruff with gratitude when I said, "Thanks, y'all. From the bottom of my heart."

"We'll stay here and come up with some possibilities, but you need to go get your man and see what's up before we start making plans," our manager said with a smile.

Xavier piped up as I pulled up flights, "Fuck, I'm so excited." Then he literally shoved me out the door as he ordered in his most jovial voice, "Everyone wish Trentham luck!"

"Good luck!" they all shouted as I stumbled onto Xavier's front walk.

Well okay then.

Chapter Ten

Enzo

It was officially spring break at the school where I was an admin, so my favorite work friends and I were out celebrating at one of Aspen's nightclubs. Riley, Marley and I were pretending that we were ritzy too, not that anyone would seriously mistake us for the rich tourists who flocked to Aspen during ski season. But we looked pretty good, and after a bunch of shots we were feeling pretty good too, grooving out on the dance floor.

We must have looked like flamingos trying to break-dance, not cool twenty-somethings, but who cared? The shots burned going down, the music was fantastic, and we were all single and ready to mingle. Or we would've been, if we weren't having so much fun.

They would've been, anyway.

I had tried dating and I'd tried hookups to get over Becker, and I had never felt worse about myself in my life. So great to learn that yeah, men were equally as dateable as women to me, but that, nope, no one else lit me up with love and joy and desire like he had.

I shook my head and danced harder.

"Oooh, is it my birthday?" Riley squealed suddenly, her eyes going huge. "Because *da-a-a-am* that is a fine-ass present wrapped up in a very big tie over there."

That had me cracking up against Marley's shoulder.

"Oh God, he's coming towards us," Marley freaked out a second later. "Enzo! Code Red!"

Straightening up, I tugged on one shoulder to resettle my shirt where it was supposed to be, rolling my eyes at their antics. But Code Red was a sacred rule in our code of friendship, so I turned around, brushing off Riley as she grabbed at my arm and pretended to swoon.

"Hey, baby."

"Did you two spike my drink with Ecstasy again?" I demanded. "We agreed: never again."

"He's not a hallucination," Marley promised, then lost all of her chill. "It is totally your brother Xavier Talon's coworker from a totally whatever, not-famous band called Downbeat. No big deal, we saw that woman with twenty million Instagram followers last month so—"

Riley hissed something, shaking her head in silent apology, and dragged Marley away.

My throat was so dry, it felt like I was gargling gravel when I swallowed.

Becker shifted his weight, looking mouth-watering in a navy button-down and black jeans straining to contain his thighs and ass, his expression strained but determined.

"Xav has one of those apps that stalks you with your permission so that no one can kidnap you," he decided to start with, "and he helped me find you because he's... helping."

I bit my lip and tried not to feel kind of proud that, despite how good he looked, he also looked even more tired and wound up than he had when he got to my door months ago. His hair hadn't been dyed since then, a few inches of dirty blond with darker silver at the roots, and his eyes were sleepy and downcast, like he hadn't rested well or thought clearly in awhile.

"Got a kidnapping threat against me, did he?" I couldn't help but tease.

"He'd have to shut up and you know he can't do that to save anyone's life," he answered, light starting to come into his eyes, his fingers uncurling from fists to rub his thighs nervously.

Nodding helplessly, I brushed my fingers over the backs of his hands.

Instantly they flipped over and grabbed me, a knuckle or two popping at the awkward angle, but I didn't care.

I'd dreamed of seeing Trentham again.

I wasn't the type of person who dreamed of rejecting him or torturing him. I couldn't hurt him even in my dreams, no matter how hard I'd cried for him and lost some of my optimism. So I'd dreamed of seeing all the loneliness I'd been feeling mirrored back at me in his dark blue gaze. I'd dreamed of him telling me everything I ever wanted to hear, love and longing and promises ripped out of him because he couldn't live without me another second.

So I just looked up at him and gave him my best smile, knowing my eyes were shining.

"Do you want to get out of here?" I asked.

Without answering, he drew me toward the exit, stopping at the coat check to get our things. He stuck his leather jacket between his knees, then held out my coat for me, and I felt my heart jump in my chest as I turned and shrugged into it. He smoothed his hands over my shoulders, then down around my ribs until he was hugging me from behind while he did up my buttons with more focus and care than I could ever have dreamed or expected from him.

It was torture when he stepped back and whipped his jacket on in a hurry, leaving it flapping open as he strode outside, towing me along happily until we were in the quiet cold.

"I—" he began, and then he tipped my chin up and searched my eyes. "Did you find someone else?" he asked in a harsh voice, but I could feel the fear behind it. "Tell me now."

A wild laugh burst out of me, and I reveled in the bite of the icy air in my lungs.

"Enzo," he warned, sharp and borderline desperate.

"Of course not!" I grabbed his waist and my eyes squeezed shut at how good it felt. These points of touch connecting us, these feelings binding us together, quick and deep like before. "But I... I tried. You were right; I needed to know if it's men I want or just... just us."

He made a rumbling noise, not a grunt like I'd gotten so used to over our short time together in January, but something closer to a purr. It made me smile a lot, though I tried to control it because he was so far out of his comfort zone and I didn't want to be mean at all.

"And?"

"Oh." I laughed again, flushing because I'd gotten so stuck on the adorable noise, I forgot to finish explaining. "Sorry, I'm so distracted. I can't believe you're here. But, no, you giant crazy person, I didn't find anyone else. I didn't really want to. I haven't been single this long since I was like fourteen and I don't miss dating at all. I've only been missing *you* and what we found."

"I think you broke me because I didn't even look—"

"Oh my God, are you Trentham? From Downbeat?" somebody screeched.

We both startled and looked over to find a group of people staring avidly at Becker.

"Yeah, I am, but you'll have to excuse me, I'm—"

"Can we get pics with you?" another one jumped in, shoving her cell towards us.

It was fascinating to watch him try to control his frustration with the awful interruption, while also maintaining his intimidating facade to encourage them to go away. "Just—"

A boldness overtook me and I ignored them, pushing up onto my toes as much as I could in my shoes, and stroked my nose up his jaw and whispered in his ear, "I love you, Becker."

"Fucking hell, Enzo," he hissed before his mouth plowed into mine, chilly and lush and so perfect. My eyes rolled back in my head as he showed me just how much he'd missed me too, while his hand supporting the back of my head felt like a little unconscious show of love.

Flashes went off behind my eyes.

I thought it was some magical love thing until Becker picked me up, twisting us around so his broad back was to the strangers who'd been after photos with him. *Photos.* He was protecting me—but he wasn't stopping the kisses, either, his erection a steel rod driving insistently against mine.

Too happy to keep more than one thought in my head, I forgot all about the strangers probably still taking pictures and watching us. Becker's kisses were life-giving, full of all of the emotions I was probably going to have to drag kicking and screaming out of him. But I didn't give a damn because I could tell he felt them, and that was all that really mattered.

By the time it registered that my fingers were freezing, he dragged his lips off of mine, steamy puffs of our frantic breaths filling up the air between our mouths. His hair was flipped the wrong way, an adorable wave falling towards one ear, and his eyes were wild.

"I'm thinking I should get to know Aspen properly," he rushed out in a raspy, desire-slurred voice. "A snowstorm wasn't the nicest way to meet her. But I really liked the way it forced me to hold still and took away any distractions. So I could start to really get to know you. But I've been a constipated ass and it's not doing anyone any good. And it turns out Chicago isn't the only place on earth where we can record our next album, did you know that?"

"Did you know that we have some pretty awesome music venues here too?" I countered, smiling so wide that my cheeks hurt, sliding my hand into his open jacket so I could press it into his hammering heart. "Our mom was a bar manager at one and she'd bring Xavier CDs from all of the bands she liked. It's a good town, and once ski season is done in about a month, it gets a tiny bit quieter, but it's never boring up here. Summer concerts, camping, disc golf..."

He dipped down until our foreheads pressed together. "I want to stay and really find out."

I angled to feather a kiss over his bottom lip. "Does it bother you that I already know?"

Quietly he admitted, "It scares me."

"That's okay, my love is pretty terrifying," I replied in my cheeriest voice. "It's really, really big and has three vicious attack animals, plus a hard nightstick it *definitely* knows how to use."

Huffing out a rough laugh, he pulled back so our eyes could meet. "I *am* ready, Enzo."

"I know you are, baby," I said a little smugly, and I liked the taste of the endearment, but I liked the way I swore it made him flush much more. "You wouldn't have come back in winter unless you were damn sure."

"Hm." He wrapped his arms around me again, and I pressed my flushed face into his chilly neck and stubbly jaw. "Xav says you better not make me as happy as you, because I'll forget to work out and I won't be the scary really hot muscular dude anymore."

"I've been researching diligently, and I think you'll make a splendid bear."

He growled again, but this time it was playful and relaxed.

"It's only a twenty-minute walk back to my place," I reassured him, giddy and happy and, yeah, cold, "and there's a spot at the end of the block that has perfect hot chocolate."

We started walking while I tugged my hat and gloves out of my coat pockets. "I don't even know what to talk about first," I admitted breathlessly. "I have so much swirling around."

"Can I stay with you while we talk about everything?" he asked after we'd gone another dozen steps. "I should get my own place, but I need to be able to see you and touch you for a week at least, I've been going crazy only having memories. I didn't even have a picture of you."

My heart tumbled joyfully in my chest and I nodded rapidly. "Yeah, yes, please."

When we got to the all-night cafe with the delicious hot chocolate, I nudged him aside and said, "I'll go in. It's a hipster place, so there's probably fans waiting to mob you."

With a disgruntled noise, he slouched against the wall, blending into the shadows.

I went in and couldn't stop grinning, and it got twice as wide when I looked out the window to check on Becker and saw him scowling as he put on some thick gloves.

"You're going to love this, here," I declared as I came back outside, handing him one.

Snow was drifting lightly down onto everything now, the lamps, signs, and traffic lights making it sparkle, coating everything in a little layer of magic. I sighed, looking up at the stars, and tipped my head against Becker's arm as we started to walk again.

"I can keep up with your long legs, you know. I want to get to my place fast and warm each other up as soon as possible, okay?"

"I know you meant that as an innuendo, but I might need to literally warm up first," he grouched. "It's still this cold in Chicago and windier, but somehow I'm *freezing* right now."

Grinning up at him, I advised sagely, "Just blame it on the altitude."

Epilogue

Trentham

Seven months later

"Hello again, my hometown! Did you miss me?" Xavier shouted while Gin jumped up and down and the full house at the intimate Aspen venue whooped and clapped.

I smiled, something I did more often and easier now, the ice that had crept around my heart long since thawed out and melted away by Enzo's bright smile and sure touches.

"Yeah, we're here to give you guys a great show tonight, but we're also here to record our next album!" Xavier went on, because he always talked too much to the crowd, not that they ever minded at all. "We'll always love Chicago, but we wanted a change of scenery, plus—"

He grunted and hopped on one foot when I kicked his heel with my boot.

"Just start singing, Xav," I suggested into the mic in an arch tone.

So he did, and off we went.

It was something we'd done a thousand times before, but tonight felt brand new. It was the first time Enzo was out there, for me. Of course he'd been to other Downbeat concerts before we got together, but those didn't count. I hadn't been in love with him then. I hadn't been aware of his presence less than fifty feet from me even though I couldn't see him because of the stage lights.

A lot of musicians I knew really got off on performing, on the energy of live audiences, giving it their all and feeding on the audiences' reactions. But I had always felt like I was simply at home, properly centered and balanced, everything in the right place. Knowing Enzo was out there, singing along off-key and dancing without an ounce of self-consciousness, made it so much more. It was transcendent, me connected to the music *and* to Enzo, this hot, sweet thing that had burst into life in the winter of a snowstorm and survived a freeze.

Between one song and the next, I heard him yell my name from somewhere in the front row and my smile made my cheeks ache, it was so big and toothy. I tossed my sweat-damp hair the way he'd admitted drove him crazy, one night this summer while we were camping. He yelled my name again, and it wasn't the same way he cried it out when we were making love, but it was in the same key. I shuddered a little, my eyes aimed at where his voice had come from, and hoped he was as turned on watching me as I was knowing he was out there.

Before I knew it, we were striding back out for the encore.

Time was, I'd hated encores. They had annoyed the crap out of me—everyone knew we were going to leave, they'd clap and shout, and we'd come back for another song or two.

This time, I was feeling like a sentimental sap and I couldn't help but compare it to a second chance, and I had a damn soft spot in my heart for them these days. I'd fucked up my heart and Enzo's by leaving Aspen, but he'd wanted to give me a second chance. It hadn't been perfect, but nothing passionate or interesting or worth fighting for ever was, was it?

Now there was nowhere else I wanted to be, no one else I wanted yelling my name.

I was ready to give that encore everything I had, take a bow, and get out of here with my one and only, forget going out with the others, I just wanted to go back to our new chalet.

So I wasn't paying as much attention to Xavier's rambling as usual.

"... a new song inspired by our once-grumpy Trentham, the best bro-in-law there is!"

My easy smile froze, and the crowd was silent for a second, then erupted in gasps.

"Damn it, Xav," I ground out, my scratchy voice coming through all the speakers.

"Oops," he said faintly.

But then I heard Enzo crack up, and I immediately relaxed and brought my hand up to shade my eyes from the stage lights, not noticing the newest ring on my fingers flashing like a beacon. When I found Enzo, he was still laughing, those beautiful eyes so bright and happy, I threw him a smile and sighed, not my old annoyed one, but a content, fulfilled sigh.

"I'm not the best with words—that's why I don't write or sing lead—but yeah, this new song is about me and my husband, Enzo, who happens to be Xav's younger brother," I told everyone. I could see all the lights on their cells as they recorded this, if they hadn't been recording the concert already, whatever. "I never would've said I was *un*happy before I felt this spark between us, but when I made the mistake of leaving instead of staying... Hell, I was in a country love song. Couldn't sleep, nothing tasted right, didn't see anyone else."

"But you came back," Enzo shouted in his happy, certain way.

"I did, baby," I agreed, "and it was the best thing your brother's ever made me do."

Everyone laughed at that, Xavier the loudest of them all, and Enzo blew me a kiss.

"Can we play the damn song and then get out of here? I've got plans later," I said.

"Happiest he's ever been, and he's still a *little* bit of a grump," Xavier mock-groused as he clapped me on the back and then started up the encore.

The song wasn't about *us*, because it would be too weird for Xavier to sing a love song on behalf of his brother and his best friend. It was about how meeting someone could change you overnight, and how it was okay to be afraid, but it wasn't okay to run away and never come back. *Some people, all they need is an arm wrapped around them, a fire to light up the night.*

When it was over, security boosted Enzo right up on stage and into my arms, and he kissed me in front of that crowd like we were all by ourselves. He didn't hold back because he didn't even know how, and while I had thought it was stupid and naive, now I knew it was brave. He was fearless, gripping the back of my neck, and I melted into him, a giant held and protected by this young, fearless man who loved me so fiercely and honestly.

"I told you he wouldn't be able to keep it a secret," Enzo whispered.

"Yeah, but I kind of like it this way," I admitted with a

low laugh, picking him up and carrying him offstage, "because now the story is about how dumb he is. It's so Xavier and so funny, and the song Seth wrote for us is so good, that I won't have to get yelled at by Kayla because I got mad and said we kept it secret because it's no one's business but ours."

Enzo smoothed a hand over my hair, his wedding ring bumping the top of my ear and making me grin because it was the only jewelry he wore. "True, but I'm glad it's all out there now. I can brag about how I'm married to a hottie rock star and you can brag about how your secret wedding was so much better—and is going to last so much longer—than your ex's!"

I couldn't help but snicker, thinking about how my ex's not-so-secret wedding had been the catalyst that had started this whole thing in the first place, and kissed Enzo again.

"I thought you're supposed to make me a better man, but that was pretty catty, baby."

The beaming smile gentled into the smile he saved just for me, that no one else got and no one else would ever get, and I swallowed hard at how it still made me feel so lucky.

"You know what I think? I think we both would've been fine if you hadn't had to hide out at my apartment. I would've been happy and you would've been good being in Downbeat. But fate helped us out and now look at us. We're so much more than we were before, not because we changed each other or made each other better, but because our hearts match."

Hugging him tight, my breaths a little ragged, I agreed hoarsely, "Yeah they do. Can we get away from all these people and go home now? I want to spend every second with you before shit gets crazy with recording and then touring. I love just being with you."

"Me too," Enzo said, smacking a kiss on my cheekbone before taking my hand and dragging me through the backstage, waving merrily at everyone but not stopping.

"But you're walking the dogs when we get home," I claimed as we got into his car.

"Only if you'll be waiting for me with hot chocolate."

"I was planning on waiting for you naked, but sure, I'll make hot chocolate instead."

As his laughter filled the car, I took his hand and kissed his ring.

———

Want to read about more musicians? Check out Ex-Bandmates!!

Acknowledgments

Thank you first to Lucy Leonnox and Leslie Copeland for organizing the Winter Wonderland 2021 giveaway and being so welcoming and supportive for newer authors like me.

Thank you to Jenny for all of her excitement for the story and for her title suggestions, and to her and my other betas Nan, Marie, and Naomi for their encouragement and help.

Thank you, as always, to my husband Matt for being the best partner and the best editor.

To all of the bloggers and readers who love romance as much as I do, thank you for taking the time to read, review, and rave! It means so much more than I can say. If you enjoyed this book, please leave a review, because you wouldn't believe how much it helps!

About the Author

Zoe writes contemporary romances and has always believed everyone will get extraordinary love stories since before she ever fell in love. She lives with her family near the mountains in Colorado, where she writes while listening to music, never drinks coffee, reads books in one sitting, and watches too many movies and tv shows. She's been writing since she was a kid, but luckily she knows how grown-ups work now. Mostly.

Follow Me!
Facebook group: Zoe's Romanceland

facebook.com/ZoeLeeBooks
twitter.com/ZoeLee_Books
instagram.com/zoe_lee_books
bookbub.com/authors/zoe-lee
goodreads.com/zoeleebooks

Want to read more romance from Zoe Lee?

Fakers (M/M)

Concocted

Fabricated (Pre-order)

Local Beats (M/M)

Ex-Bandmates

Ex-Daredevil

Ex-Rivals

Ex-Beefcake

Maybelle County (M/F)

Pour Your Heart Out

Fifteen Nights

A Perfect Fit

Hidden Tracks